# *The Pink Pumpkin Party*

## A Witch's Cove Mystery
## Book 7

## Vella Day

The Pink Pumpkin Party
Copyright © 2020 by Vella Day
Print Edition
www.velladay.com
velladayauthor@gmail.com

Cover Art by Jaycee DeLorenzo
Edited by Rebecca Cartee and Carol Adcock-Bezzo

Published in the United States of America

Print book ISBN: 978-1-951430-22-1

ALL RIGHTS RESERVED. No part of this book may be used or reproduced in any manner whatsoever without written permission of the author except in the case of brief questions embodied in critical articles or reviews.

This is a work of fiction. Names, characters, places, and incidents either are the product of the author's imagination or are used fictitiously, and any resemblance to actual persons living or dead, business establishments, events or locales, is entirely coincidental.

**How can a perfectly planned Halloween party go really, really wrong? Easy. A dead body shows up in my decorated coffin. Welcome to my witchy world.**

Hi, I'm Glinda Goodall, the good witch from the south, who is a hopeless snoop turned amateur sleuth. I had one job this October, and that was to decorate for the annual Halloween fest at my aunt's restaurant. It was organized to the max: ghosts floating on the ceiling, a coffin with a vampire, and a small cemetery surrounded by pink painted pumpkins. Spooky yet festive.

Just my luck, someone was murdered at the party. I might not have inserted myself into the investigation had the corpse not been a very important person to our family. At first, it seemed like an open and was whether our friend was the intended victim or not.

With the help from my psychic cousin and my talented computer expert business partner, we're sure to get to the bottom of this. So, stop in at the Tiki Hut Grill for a cup of java, and you just might see me.

## Chapter One

"YOU WANT *ALL* of the pumpkins painted pink?" Rihanna asked.

I chuckled at her horror. "Are you suggesting a few get a splash of black?"

"You know that Halloween should have more representation than just pink," my cousin said with a teenage rebellious tone.

I understood where she was coming from. Halloween was synonymous with orange and black. "Fine. We can have some unpainted orange ones and a few black ones."

Rihanna grinned. "You are the best."

I chuckled. "Keep painting."

Let me explain my cousin's comment—and my response. First of all, my name is Glinda Goodall, named after the movie character Glinda, the Good Witch from the South, and I live in Witch's Cove, Florida, a small beach town full of witches, psychics, fortune tellers, and a few werewolves tossed in for good measure.

After deciding that being a math teacher wasn't my thing, I moved home and took a job as a waitress in my aunt's restaurant, the Tiki Hut Grill. All was well for a few years until Jaxson Harrison, the brother of my best male friend,

Drake, returned to town. Jaxson was not only hot—as in great to look at—he was hot-headed. No doubt about it, our newcomer was definitely trouble.

When our deputy was murdered, Jaxson became our number one suspect since he'd just finished serving three years in jail for supposedly robbing a liquor store. Naturally, I had to help Drake prove his brother wasn't the killer.

That intervention led to a series of events that ended with me and Jaxson starting The Pink Iguana Sleuths. Shock, I know. To be honest, I can't keep my nose out of anything, and as it turns out, I'm actually quite good at solving murder cases—with the help of our sheriff's department, of course. I lucked out, because Jaxson is a genius when it comes to doing research. I swear the man can find anything on the computer. Oh, yeah. If you haven't guessed, Jaxson wasn't guilty of any crime. He'd been framed.

So, what did this history lesson have to do with painting Halloween pumpkins pink? And why was my eighteen-year old cousin helping me?

That's easy. Except when duty calls—that is, when I'm on a case—I only wear pink, which was why I was painting the pumpkins that distinctive color. However, Rihanna only wears black since she has a need to express herself, too. As for why my eighteen-year old cousin was helping me instead of being back in Tallahassee where she lived? That was simple, too. After years of drug abuse, Rihanna's mother finally decided to enter rehab, which meant my cousin needed a place to stay for a few months. After some debate, she moved here. She's now living in a room off of our office. And by *our office*, I mean the one I share with my business partner—turned potential boyfriend—Jaxson. Can you understand why I had to fill you in? My life is complicated.

I'm glad she's here, because Rihanna is quite a talented psychic. In fact, in the two months since her arrival, my cousin has helped solve a few crimes.

"Did you finish the vampire for the coffin?" she asked.

"Almost." My parents own the funeral home that sits next to the Tiki Hut Grill where tomorrow night's party will be held. "I'm still working on the face. I've made it out of papier-mâché, and I just need to paint the fangs and eyes."

"Cool. And the graveyard?"

I was impressed that my cousin had been listening to my plans to make this the best Halloween party ever. "I'm using the same gravestones we used last year. They're made out of Styrofoam, but they look real."

Rihanna grabbed a pink pumpkin whose paint had dried and added black eyeliner, long eyelashes, and black lips. I—the woman who loved pink—was willing to admit that her artwork improved the pink pumpkin greatly.

My cell rang. "It's Jaxson."

He and his brother, Drake, were in charge of renting and then setting up the projector that would splash the image of ghosts on the restaurant ceiling. Tomorrow, my father's crew would carry over the coffin with the vampire inside.

My body sagged at all that needed to be done by then. I don't know why I allowed my Aunt Fern to talk me into doing this event this year. Sure, Halloween—and maybe Christmas—were my favorite holidays, but it took a lot out of me to make this *the* big happening of the year.

Thankfully—or not so thankfully—no one had been

murdered in Witch's Cove since the beginning of September, which meant I had the time to devote to this endeavor.

That didn't mean Jaxson and I had no clients. We'd been hired to follow one husband to see why he came home late two days a week. Naturally, the wife was convinced he was having an affair. Was he? No. Turns out, he was taking dance lessons to surprise her on their anniversary. Was that sweet or what?

And then there was the case of the stolen wedding gown. In that instance, the woman's twenty-two-year-old daughter had forgotten to tell her mother that she needed to lend it to her best friend for her wedding.

As much as these small jobs brought in some needed cash, it didn't give me the rush that a good old-fashioned murder did. However, if too many people died in Witch's Cove, our tourism rate might go down.

"I'm done," Rihanna announced.

"Great." We were sitting in the alley between the Tiki Hut Grill and The Cove Mortuary. Not wanting anyone to come by and steal our fine artwork, I'd waited until the pumpkins had almost dried before moving them inside. "I'm going to carry the rest of these to the storage room."

"I'll wait here."

"Thanks." One by one, I placed the finished masterpieces on one of the cleared storage room shelves.

After the last delivery, Rihanna gathered the remaining supplies. "What did you finally decide to wear for the party?" she asked.

I had gone back and forth many times, but the costume shop in town had limited choices, and I didn't want to ask my

Aunt Fern to make me one. I'd done that too many times in the past. "I'm going as Supergirl, and Jaxson will be Superman."

"Ooh. I'd like to see that man in a tight outfit."

"Rihanna Samuels. No lustful thoughts. Besides, you have your own cutie to watch."

Heat raced up her face. "I do at that."

"What are you and Gavin going as?"

She shrugged. "I thought about wearing a Fairy costume with blue wings and all, but then I couldn't bring myself to put it on. I caved and gave into my need for black."

"Don't tell me you're going as a vampire?"

"Guilty. Not original, I know, but if I can't drink, I want to be comfortable."

I chuckled. "And Gavin?"

"His sense of humor seriously deteriorated once he started working for his mom in the morgue—or so he says. Gavin is going as a zombie, and I, for one, am looking forward to doing his makeup."

"I thought you'd go as a couple. As in, you'd match."

"Matching is tacky. I mean, it is except for someone your age."

"Seriously? I'm only eight years older than you."

"Just saying."

I understood her concern, but Jaxson was okay with it. "Let's finish putting these supplies away. Then I want to check with Aunt Fern to make sure there isn't something else she needs me to do."

AFTER DONNING MY costume the next evening, I kind of felt silly when I looked in the mirror. Supergirl? What had I been thinking? I wore a costume when I waitressed, but going as my Glinda the Good Witch persona wouldn't be in the Halloween spirit. Picking a super hero didn't fit my personality either, but Jaxson had suggested it. Why I listened to him, I don't know, though it could have been because I was always calling him my superman.

Iggy waddled into the bedroom and looked up at me. "Can I come to the party?"

Iggy was my pink, super sleuth iguana. He's also my familiar, and we've been together about fifteen years. "There will be food, music, and alcohol. To be honest, I don't trust anyone to pay enough attention not to step on you."

"You know I can stay out of the way. And I have that camouflaged outfit that Aunt Fern made for me."

"That is a costume, for sure, but it will make you more susceptible to being hurt." So what if he could stick to the wall?

Before he could come up with another argument, a knock sounded on my door. "That's Jaxson." I rushed out of my bedroom, and when I answered it, I sucked in a breath. "Wow. You look great."

He grinned, stepped inside, and kissed me. "Let me see your costume."

I spun around, a bit self-conscious. I was chunky and probably should have gone as a ghost and worn a white sheet to cover my curves. "It's a little tight."

"Are you kidding? You look great." He looked over at Iggy. "Why aren't you dressed, bud?"

"See?" my sassy iguana tossed back. "Jaxson wants me to go."

I knew when I was defeated. "Okay, but don't get in anyone's way."

He did his circle dance of joy. "I won't."

His costume was in my bedroom closet. Once I retrieved it, I put it on him. I had to admit, he looked cute. "Do you want some green face paint?"

"Yes, please. I'd like to look normal at least one day a year."

"No one will think you're special if you're green, you know." I loved the fact that he was pink.

"I'm good with that. Maybe no one will recognize me."

"Sure, they will. How many other iguanas have you seen in this town?"

"A lot. Okay, a few."

More like none. It didn't matter. I just wanted Iggy to be happy. "And Aimee? Won't she feel left out?"

Iggy stared at me. "I guess, but she can't get out of the way like I can."

Aimee was a cat that Aunt Fern had adopted. By mistake, this cat had been given the gift of speech. If I had to guess, Iggy used the idea she might be trampled on as an excuse not to invite her. My familiar loved to be the special one at a party.

Someone knocked on my aunt's door across the hall from my apartment. It probably was her new boyfriend, Peter Upton. I didn't know much about the man, but he made my aunt happy, and that's what was important.

I turned to Jaxson. "We have the first shift. Ready?"

"You bet."

I'd already checked that the decorations around the restaurant were all set to go. Aunt Fern had closed the Tiki Hut two hours ago to allow some service workers to clear out the tables and chairs, and I couldn't wait for everyone to see what we'd accomplished.

As promised, my dad's crew had delivered the coffin. With the red light focused on the interior, I had to say the vampire looked so real it almost creeped me out.

Jaxson and Drake had set up the projector that would shine the ghosts on the ceiling. Add in the pumpkins and the fans blowing dry ice over the cemetery, and the Tiki Hut Grill had been transformed into a scary but magical wonderland.

To further enhance the ambiance, Aunt Fern insisted we buy a few mannequins and dress them in locally themed Halloween costumes. Since Witch's Cove was situated on the Gulf of Mexico, she'd dressed one in a shark outfit. Yes, she has a warped sense of humor. Dave Sanders, the owner of the Witch's Cove Dive Shop, lent us his mannequin who was wearing a diving suit. To make the evening even more fun, Aunt Fern had hired a live band.

We'd set up two tables—one out in front of the restaurant and one in back—to collect the party fee of twenty dollars. The money covered one trip to the buffet and two drinks. The Fire Marshall said we had to keep total attendance to one hundred people or less, which meant we needed to communicate with the table in back to make sure we didn't go over our limit.

Jaxson and I had signed up to take the first shift in front, because it was the most hectic time. Jaxson would handle the money and place a white band on the person's wrist, while I would hand out the food and drink tokens after checking the IDs, if necessary.

I nudged him. "Here comes the sheriff. Or at least I think that is Steve." He was wearing a Captain Hook costume, complete with a large hat, fake mustache, and an eyepatch. His date, who I believe was Misty Willows, the sheriff over in Liberty, came dressed as Peter Pan. They looked really cute together.

"Glinda, Jaxson," the sheriff said. "Forty for the two of us, right?"

"That's right." Jaxson took the money, while I pressed my clicker twice and then handed them their tokens. "Enjoy the party."

I didn't have to check their IDs since I knew who they were. The next group had costumes that covered their faces. One wore a Spiderman costume, another was Batman, and a third was Olaf from the movie *Frozen*. I checked their drivers' licenses and had to assume they belonged to the person holding the card. Considering their rather muscled bodies, they weren't high school kids. "Have fun."

"Thanks, little lady." That deep voice definitely belonged to an adult male.

Just as I turned to say something to Jaxson, a second wave of people arrived. First in line were Miriam and Maude Daniels, who were dressed as Raggedy Ann and Andy. They, too, looked adorable. Right behind them was Rihanna and Gavin. At five feet ten inches, my cousin made a rather imposing vampire.

"The white face makeup and heavy black eye makeup are

perfect," I said. As was the black cape and red vest over the white shirt.

"Thanks. I had fun with it." She flashed me her fangs.

"Sweet."

I checked out Gavin. His outfit made him almost unrecognizable. Rihanna had done a great job making him look like he had real cuts and bruises on his face. I handed them their buffet and soft drink tokens and told them to enjoy the party.

For the next forty-five minutes, we had a non-stop flow of people. While I had thought Deputy Nash Solano would dress up as a werewolf, since he was one in real life, he chose to come as a vampire, too. While his costume matched Rihanna's, he didn't have nearly the same amount of black eyeliner that she did. "I like the fangs, but you might have a hard time enjoying our buffet with them in."

He winked. "Trust me, I'll take them out." Nash fished out his money, and I gave him the tokens in exchange.

Once he stepped inside, two of our evening servers came outside. "You guys can go in and have some fun. We'll take over."

I handed her the clicker. "Just let the person at the back know when you reach fifty."

"Will do."

We both stood. I couldn't wait for my first dance with Jaxson. Tonight was going to be epic.

## Chapter Two

THE GHOSTS FLOATING on the ceiling of the Tiki Hut Grill, the red lights that bathed the coffin, and the dry ice surrounding the small cemetery created an otherworldly feeling. The restaurant never looked better.

"You and your aunt really pulled out all of the stops."

"Thanks."

Jaxson nodded to the couple across the room. "Speaking of your aunt, she and her date sure look happy."

Peter was in the same vampire costume as Rihanna. Ten bucks said she did his makeup since it looked like hers. As for Aunt Fern, she was wearing a 1920's flapper outfit. The Mary Jane heels and the headband with attached feather added the perfect touch.

For the next few minutes, I checked out the other costumes. My mom wore her usual one—that of Dorothy from *The Wizard of Oz*. I was happy she had a stuffed Toto in her basket instead of her real dog. Last year, she'd brought Toto who barked so much, my mom had to take her home.

As for Dad? He came as the Scarecrow. Last year he'd come as the cowardly lion, and the year before that as the Wizard of Oz. He said the Tin Man suit was too uncomfortable, and I could totally understand that.

Penny and Hunter rushed up to us. "You look amazing. Glinda, I am so proud of you for dressing up as Supergirl. And to think your outfit is not pink!"

Heat raced up my face. "I've been working on getting out of my pink rut, but I don't ever plan to go mainstream."

"I should hope not." Penny looked over at Superman. "Looking good, Clark."

"Back at you, Little Red Riding Hood."

I almost chuckled at Hunter's choice as the big bad wolf. It was appropriate since he, too, was a werewolf—something very few people were aware of.

Jaxson placed a hand on my back. "Care to dance?"

They were playing a relatively slow song, and it shot me back to my high school prom when Drake and I went together. It was a shame that Jaxson's brother couldn't come to the party tonight, but Saturday night at the wine shop was his busiest time. "I'd love to."

While we spent every day together, Jaxson and I had only gone out on two official dates. Both had ended in a kiss, but I was hoping this party might take us to the next level. While some might say this atmosphere was less than romantic, to me, it was ideal.

Jaxson loosely wrapped both arms around my waist, and I lifted my hands to his shoulders. "When was the last time you danced?" he asked.

That was a hard one. "I can't even remember."

He smiled. "Me, neither."

Jaxson pulled me close, and I decided to forget all of my worries for the next few minutes and just enjoy myself. I placed my cheek on his chest and let the music enter my soul.

All too soon, someone tapped on Jaxson's shoulder. Ugh. I looked up at the intruder. It was my dad! To say I was shocked would be an understatement.

"May I have this dance?" he asked.

"I'd like that."

Jaxson nodded and handed me over. Dad lifted my right hand in his left, and I placed my free hand on his shoulder—all very proper stuff.

"Are you having fun?" I asked him. He rarely left the funeral home.

"All is good," he said and then smiled.

I wasn't sure what that was about until he removed his right hand from around my waist and wiggled his finger. Oh, my. He was wearing a new garnet ring. "Is that what I think it is?"

"Yup. Nash and Hunter came through with the magic ring. There are now five turned-against-their-will werewolves who are safe from ever being affected by the full moon."

"That's fantastic."

Quick catch up on how my dad became a werewolf in the first place. Because the local werewolf clan believed I had the magic to create rings that would help them control their shift, they turned my father into a werewolf in the hopes I'd make these rings for them. Unfortunately, they were sorely mistaken. I didn't possess that talent, but Nash and Hunter knew someone who did. They'd promised to find a way to end my dad's need to shift, and now they had delivered on their promise.

The song finished. "Thanks for the dance, Dad. I enjoyed it."

My father never was the overtly affectionate type, so when he leaned over and kissed my forehead, I was elated. "Me, too, sweetie."

As soon as my father blended into the crowd—or as much as a scarecrow could blend in—Jaxson returned to my side. "We should grab that buffet before it's picked over."

I doubted Aunt Fern would let that happen, but he understood I could always eat. "Good idea."

Other than the few tables that held some finger foods, the inside was devoid of any place to sit. Once we filled up our plate, we headed to the back porch where the tables were located and grabbed one near the back.

Next to the beachside Tiki Hut, Aunt Fern had set up a cauldron on the sand over an open fire that had red-colored water in it that looked like bubbling blood. Its appearance was quite authentic. Off to the side sat an apple-bobbing stand, but no one was taking advantage of it—at least not yet.

And then there was the Tiki Hut bar itself, where every stool was occupied. It was no wonder considering both cute bartenders were dressed as pirates, complete with black headbands and eye patches. I thought their red and black striped pants were a bit too tight, but the women seated there probably appreciated them.

I was halfway through my meal when a rather hunched over homeless woman sauntered onto the porch. She had on her white wristband, so she was a paid party goer. "Is that Dolly?" I whispered to Jaxson. She ran the Spellbound Diner and was one of my go-to gossip queens.

"It could be, but it's too dark to be sure."

As soon as the woman opened the door to head inside, the

music poured out onto the porch.

Ray Zink, one of the evening shift workers at the Tiki Hut, got up from behind his table and came over. "Hey, Glinda. We've reached our one-hundred-person limit."

"That was fast. How about putting up the sign that says the party is closed?" I'd laminated one sheet for the front and one for the back that were designed to slip into the display slots.

He smiled. "Will do."

"What is to prevent anyone from sneaking in?" Jaxson asked.

"Probably not much, but they can't have any drinks unless they pay for them directly."

"How about we finish our meal and sit inside the front door to make sure no one else comes in? We can ask the bartenders back here to tell anyone without a wristband they can't enter."

"We don't have to be door monitors, you know. That can't be fun for you."

Jaxson smiled. "As long as we're together, I'm happy."

Aw. "Then thank you."

Before we went back inside, I asked the bartenders to keep an eye on the rear entrance.

"We'll try, but it gets a bit busy back here."

"Do what you can."

I was hoping the sign would be sufficient to keep people out, but not everyone would bother to read it.

Once we reached the main entrance, we carried the outside table and chairs into the restaurant. I then sat down.

"I'll grab us something to drink," he said. "What would

you like?"

"Surprise me."

Sitting here might be boring for Jaxson, but I, for one, loved to people watch. Some of the costumes had clearly been handmade, while others had purchased theirs. Trying to guess who was behind some of the masks would be fun.

"Here ya go." Jax handed me a beer.

"Thank you. Have you seen Dr. Sanchez?"

She was Gavin's mom and our medical examiner. Elissa Sanchez was an attractive single woman who shouldn't be sitting home on such a festive evening. Halloween wasn't until tomorrow, but having our party tonight allowed everyone to be home to hand out candy when the kids came knocking.

"No, but I imagine Gavin gave her strict instructions not to spoil his date."

I chuckled. "You're probably right."

I had wondered if it would bother me having my parents here when I was with Jaxson, but I was pleased to say it didn't.

Something crashed off to the side and startled me. The music continued, but many of the guests turned to rubberneck, as did I. "I probably should see if anything needs to be cleaned up."

"I'll help you."

We left our drinks on the table and headed over to where we usually kept the condiment table, because the noise came from over there. Several paper platefuls of food were on the floor, as were a few spilled drinks. As a former teacher, I was about to ask who'd done this, but then I realized no one would confess.

I looked around for Iggy, but it was too dark to see much

of anything. "I'll get the mop," I told Jaxson.

"Where do you keep the trash bags?"

"In the kitchen."

I hadn't taken more than three steps when the power went out. "Are you kidding me?"

With the electricity off, the music stopped, which seemed to cause the talking to escalate. At that moment, I envied my dad, Nash, and Hunter since their werewolf eyesight would enable them to see in the dark. About the only light that entered the restaurant came from the streetlights. I found it odd that they were on considering our power was out.

Someone on the other side of the room groaned and then cursed. Even over the din of the crowd, I'd heard the sounds, which officially freaked me out. I wasn't claustrophobic or anything, but I didn't like being in the dark. "Jaxson?"

Someone grabbed my arm. "I'm here. Where is the electrical panel?"

He never seemed upset over anything, and I really appreciated that he had a clear head in times of trouble. "It's in the closet in back."

Jaxson turned on his phone's flashlight. That was smart. I would have brought mine if my outfit had a pocket to hold my cell. So, where had he kept his? And why hadn't other people turned theirs on?

Before I could come up with an answer, a door banged shut, but it was hard to figure out what was going on with all of the shuffling of feet and murmuring.

Jaxson tugged my arm. "Come on. I don't want to leave you by yourself."

That was sweet of him. Rihanna had Gavin to keep her

safe, my aunt had Peter, and most of the people had come with a guest. I hurried down the hallway toward the closet. Once inside the room, Jaxson threw some switch, and the lights magically appeared.

"Thank goodness," I said.

He faced me. "Someone did this."

My stomach plummeted. "What do you mean?"

"Unless I am wrong, someone tampered with the master switch. They wanted to cut the power."

That made no sense. "Why?"

He tapped my nose. "We won't find out standing here."

Jaxson pushed open the door just as a scream rippled down the hallway, causing my pulse to skyrocket. "That sounds like Aunt Fern."

I took off at a dead run. When I reached the main room, I couldn't see her, but I heard her wails of pain near the corner where the coffin was located. A crowd had gathered around the area, so I couldn't see what was going on.

Jaxson grabbed my arm. "Stay here."

"No way. Aunt Fern is the one crying."

He hesitated. "Fine, but we go together."

Before we reached her, Steve and Nash blocked our path. "Everyone, please stay back."

Only after most of the people had moved out of the way did I see there was another body in the coffin. Oh. My. Goodness. He, or maybe she, was wearing a vampire outfit, and my mind blanked.

"Rihanna?" I managed to eke out, my heart pumping hard. She had been dressed as a vampire.

Someone rushed in through the back door. It was Rihanna and Gavin, and my heart slowed down a bit.

"Make way, people." Nash motioned for everyone to clear a path so he could help my aunt to a chair.

I ran over to her. "Aunt Fern. What happened? Are you okay?"

She shook her head. "It's Peter."

I wasn't very good in a crisis. My mind often couldn't put the pieces together. "What about Peter?"

"Someone killed him."

"What?"

It suddenly dawned on me that he, too, had come as a vampire. I wanted to ask if she was sure he was dead, but Steve would have called an ambulance if her date was merely drunk or injured. As much as I wanted to check it out, I had to stay by my aunt's side.

A moment later, Jaxson held out a glass of water. "You should drink this," he said to her.

"Thank you." She took a few sips. "Why would anyone kill Peter?" my aunt choked out.

"I have no idea, but maybe he wasn't the intended target. He looked like…Rihanna…and Nash and a few others." I had no idea how many had come dressed as a vampire. I also wasn't sure if mentioning that would make her grief better or worse. In retrospect, I probably should have kept my mouth shut.

Steve grabbed the band's microphone. "Everyone, please. Nobody leave. I know a terrible event has occurred, but we need to ask you all a few questions. I'm hoping one of you saw something."

The back door opened, and the two outside bartenders

ushered in a bunch of people—a few of which I recognized from having been seated at the outside bar.

Steve motioned me and Jaxson over. "Can you two stand watch at the front to make sure no one enters or leaves?"

"Sure."

"I'll ask Penny and Hunter to keep watch on the back door," he said.

My heart still hadn't stopped pounding. "Is Peter really dead?"

Steve pressed his lips together. "I'm afraid so. And no, I don't know the cause of death, but I've texted Dr. Sanchez. Nash is on his way to the department to grab our crime scene tape and fingerprint material."

Misty, Steve's date, was by his side. "I'll call in my team, too. We'll help you find the person who did this."

"Thank you." For once, I wasn't trying to figure out what I could do to solve this crime. I just wanted to be there for my aunt.

The bag lady came closer. Oh, my. It was Dolly, only now she was no longer hunched over. "Sheriff, may I have a word?"

"Did you see something?"

"I believe I did."

His brows rose. "Yes?"

She stepped closer. "I saw Spiderman approach the vampire. He had what looked like your Captain's hook in his hand."

Steve's eyes widened, and then he glanced over to the check-out counter. "Oh, no. I set the prop down over there so I could eat. Someone must have picked it up."

Jaxson clasped my shoulders. "Glinda, we need to guard

the door."

My mother and father were escorting Aunt Fern upstairs, probably against her will, but she didn't need to see what would happen next.

"Of course."

What had started out as maybe the best night of my life, had turned into the worst.

## Chapter Three

THE NEXT NINETY minutes were surreal. Steve, Nash, and Misty questioned everyone. They took names, phone numbers, and even snapped everyone's picture. While I couldn't hear much of what was going on, no one seemed to have known the deceased very well—other than Aunt Fern.

I was thankful that Steve wasn't questioning her regarding her boyfriend's murder. From her distraught reaction, my aunt had nothing to do with his death.

I made my way over to Steve. "How many people in total did you question?"

"A lot."

"We were only allowed to have one hundred people in here. I'm wondering if perhaps the killer was able to escape in all of the chaos."

"Let me check."

Steve counted his names. "I have seventy." He turned to Misty to compare their two lists. "How many do you have?"

"Twenty-seven, including the band members and other staff."

"Are you counting me, Jaxson, or Aunt Fern?"

"I did. That means our killer should be one of these people."

"That's a scary thought," I said.

"No kidding," Steve said.

I looked over at the coffin where Gavin and his mom were doing their preliminary work. "Peter was no lightweight. Unless he crawled into the coffin himself and then was killed, I doubt a woman could have pulled this off."

"Agreed, unless she had an accomplice."

There was that. "Why are murder cases always so complicated?" Yes, it was a rhetorical question.

Steve clasped my shoulder. "Glinda, I know that you'll want to help because it is your aunt's boyfriend. While I appreciate it, you need to sit this one out."

Did he think I'd mess things up? "This is my aunt we're talking about. She and Peter were tight. I'm not sure when or if she'll recover, which is why I have to do something."

If possible, Steve looked more distressed. "How long has she known him?"

"Only a few weeks, but they really clicked."

"What did Peter do for a living?"

I sucked in a breath, trying to dredge up a memory. "Finance, maybe? I honestly don't remember, but something has been bothering me about his death."

"What's that?"

"Did you know that Rihanna did his makeup?"

"No, but what does that have to do with anything?"

"Peter was the same height as Rihanna. What if she had been the target? It would be easy to get the wrong person. It was dark in here."

"Glinda." I didn't like his patronizing tone.

"What? It's possible. Or maybe the killer was after Nash.

He came as a vampire, don't forget. Ever think about that?"

"Or the killer could have been after the other vampire, assuming I didn't miss one. Are we to delve into each of their lives?"

I wasn't sure if I wanted to answer that question. "Maybe. Who was the fourth person?"

"Levy Poole."

Dread attacked my stomach. Levy was a very powerful, but good, warlock. "Levy was here? I didn't see him."

Steve shrugged. "He might have come in the back entrance while you were taking money in the front."

"Maybe."

"Look, Glinda. We will consider your theory that Mr. Upton wasn't the target, but regardless, there is a murderer out there that we need to find."

"Which is exactly why I want to help. Rihanna and Levy foiled that coven's plan to rob all those safes last month. Either one might now be a target."

Nash entered the restaurant without his vampire cape and set the crime scene gear near the coffin. He was a little shorter than Rihanna. While he was quite broad shouldered, the cape and large collar would have blocked a lot of his body's shape. Personally, I'd put my money on Rihanna being the target, but I hoped I was wrong. "I'm betting your deputy has made a few enemies since coming here."

"I'm sure he has."

This conversation wasn't getting me anywhere. "I need to check on my aunt."

"Good idea, and remember, this is *our* case."

Even though I wanted to salute him, I didn't. "I know.

How much longer are you going to be?"

Steve looked around. "Maybe another half hour. Why?"

"I need to lock up." The band had already packed up their gear and were about to head out. "Can you text me when you're about to leave?"

"Sure thing."

Since Rihanna's boyfriend was busy with the body, Jaxson was keeping her company, for which I was glad. The three of us should stick together in this time of need. I headed over to them. "Hi."

"Did you learn anything?" Jaxson asked.

"Other than all one-hundred people were accounted for? No."

Rihanna shivered. "That means the killer was still here when the lights came on."

"It appears so."

I debated bringing up my theory that Peter Upton might not have been the target but now wasn't the time. "Did you have the chance to talk to Levy?"

She smiled briefly. "I did."

"Before or after the tragedy?"

"Both."

Something was going on. "What aren't you telling me?"

She reached out and ran a hand down my arm. "Don't worry. I can take care of myself if I was the intended target. We know Levy probably can't be caught. I mean, he can cloak himself and become invisible."

I was glad about that. "Did Levy think Peter Upton might not have been the intended target either?" That would confirm my hypothesis.

"Yes, but he said there are always disgruntled people in his coven. Since he is their leader, someone always tries to take him down. Thankfully, no one has succeeded."

If the killer had been after Levy, he'd be the hardest of the four to kill. "We'll have to get Steve to show him the list of names of the people who were in attendance to see if he recognizes any of them."

She shrugged. "I guess."

I wish I could read her mind, but her body posture implied she was worried, for which I was thankful. She might take more care. At least when she was in school, she'd be safe. As much as I'd like to suggest that Jaxson or I drive her each way, Rihanna wouldn't stand for it. She was of legal age and a witch. Then again, Peter Upton was an adult, and he was dead.

"Glinda, how about we see to your aunt?" Jaxson said.

"Yes, of course. My parents are with her, but I'm sure she'd appreciate our company. First, though, I need to find Iggy."

"I saw him go upstairs a while ago," Rihanna said.

"That's good to know." I hope he wasn't too traumatized by all of this.

The three of us went up to my aunt's apartment. I knocked lightly and then entered. My aunt was sitting on the sofa with Iggy and Aimee perched on her lap. Dad was next to her, and my mom was sitting on the chair across from them.

My mom looked up. "Any news?"

"No."

My aunt had stopped crying, but she was far from okay. I rushed over to the sofa and knelt in front of her. "Hey."

"Oh, Glinda." She grabbed my hand.

"Don't worry, Steve is working hard to find out who did this."

She nodded. "I'm sure he is."

"I need to get the door keys and lock up once everyone leaves."

"I hadn't even thought of that, but yes. The keys are on the table in the kitchen."

I rushed over there and snatched them. Both Jaxson and Rihanna took a seat across from her. Asking Aunt Fern questions at a time like this wasn't ideal, but the quicker we could learn why Peter was dead, the better chance we had at finding the killer—or rather of Steve finding who did this. "Did Peter ever say he might be in danger?"

My aunt looked up at me, and swiped a finger under her eyes. "No."

"Can you think of any reason why someone would kill him, assuming he was the target?"

"Everyone loved him. He gave start-up businesses money to expand."

I hadn't been aware he was a venture capitalist. That implied he was rather wealthy, which meant someone in his family might have wanted him dead. "Did he have any children?"

"Yes. Two grown sons, but they live in New York."

They could have flown down to Florida in order to attend the party. However, their own father would have recognized them unless they had worn an outfit that covered their faces. Steve would have their names though. Even if they used fake ones, I bet Jaxson could locate a family picture and compare it to those who had attended our soiree.

"Does Peter have an office in town?"

"Glinda," my mother said. "Can the interrogation wait until later?"

She was right. I told myself I wanted to be supportive of my aunt in her time of need, and what was I doing? Acting like I was a real detective. "Of course. I'm sorry. I'm just trying to help."

My aunt looked up at me. "I know you are." She squeezed her brother-in-law's hand. "If you all don't mind, I'd like to lie down."

That was our cue to leave. "I'll lock up and then drop the keys through the cat door."

"Thank you, Glinda."

We all left—including Iggy. Because it was only about ten, I was hoping I could convince Jaxson to brainstorm what might have happened here tonight.

"After I close up, I want to stop back at the office. Jaxson, will you come with us?"

"Of course."

"I'm coming too," Iggy said.

"Okay. Let me grab my purse." I stepped into my apartment and retrieved it. "Hop in, buddy."

The four of us headed downstairs. Gavin and his mom were gone, and the corpse was no longer in the coffin. Only the police tape remained as a cruel reminder of what happened here.

I wasn't sure when the Tiki Hut Grill would be allowed to open for business. It could take a long time to dust the place for prints—assuming that was what Steve planned to do.

"There you are," Steve said. "I was just about to text you. We're heading out."

"Tell me what I can and can't touch."

"I'd like to keep the restaurant closed tomorrow, but I won't force the issue if your aunt wants to open up. As for putting away the decorations, if you could keep away from the coffin area, that would be great."

"I can do that. The plan had been to wait until lunchtime to open anyway since we need to clean up and then return the tables and chairs, which will take time."

"I'll keep that in mind," Steve said.

After I locked up, Rihanna, Jaxson, and I walked back to the office. I wanted to escort Rihanna back there anyway, because I had the sick feeling that she might be the next target. If we had any family back in Jacksonville, I would have suggested she return there.

Once inside, Iggy climbed out of my purse. "I saw something," he announced.

"Why didn't you say anything before?"

"I didn't think it was important at the time."

"Hold that thought, bud. I need some coffee. Anyone else want a cup?" Jaxson asked.

"Sure." I doubted I was going to get much sleep tonight anyway.

"I'll help," Rihanna said.

Both of them headed toward the kitchen area. I looked down at Iggy. "Sit next to me so I can take off your costume. It can't be all that comfortable."

"It's not."

I removed his camouflaged outfit but decided to leave on

the green face paint until tomorrow. Washing his face, hands, and legs took too much time.

A few minutes later, Jaxson and Rihanna returned with a tray of coffee and some cookies. My mouth watered. "You guys are the best."

Jaxson smiled. "We try."

They both sat down. "We're ready, bud. What do you want to tell us?"

## Chapter Four

"I SAW THREE guys sneak out of the party after the lights went out. I have good eyesight, you know." Iggy puffed out his chest.

How was that possible if all one-hundred people were accounted for? "Where were you when you saw this?"

"I was behind the counter where Aunt Fern usually stands. It was about the only safe place where I wouldn't get trampled."

I gained no satisfaction knowing I'd been right in warning him how dangerous it could be. "How do you know they'd been at the party?" I asked.

"They were carrying costumes."

Carrying them? "That makes no sense. No one goes to a party and then puts on a costume."

"Maybe they were at the party, left, and changed in the alley. Strange for sure, but it's possible," Jaxson said. "They then returned to their car and took off. They could have had another engagement that didn't require costumes."

"No," Iggy said.

"What do you mean, bud?" Jaxson asked.

"I saw them toss Spiderman costumes into their car and then head back in the direction of the side alley. I thought it odd that three friends would dress alike in the first place."

My mind spun at what that might mean. "Do you think they returned after the lights went out. I heard a door slam."

"I don't know," he said. "I'm just reporting to you what I saw."

I changed focus. "Okay, if they were headed back toward the water, it's possible they just went for a walk on the beach." Farfetched, I know.

"I didn't pay attention once Aunt Fern started screaming."

I wasn't sure what to make of it. "Were they wearing white wristbands?"

"I don't know," Iggy said.

I wasn't sure his account helped, but I'd have to remember to tell Steve when I saw him next. "That's okay. We'll figure it out."

Three men in street clothes would stand out. Considering Steve took a photo of everyone, these men would be easy to spot.

"Does this mean we're investigating the murder?" Rihanna asked.

"No," Jaxson and I answered simultaneously.

"Why not?"

Unless I worked at blocking my thoughts, Rihanna had the ability to read my mind—or at least, bits and pieces of it. Right now, my thoughts were rather jumbled, which probably prevented her from catching more than a few random words. "We can't be certain that whoever killed Peter Upton is finished."

She shook her head. "You're still hung up on the idea this

guy may come after me or Levy?"

"Well, you two did disrupt the plans of some of those coven members. Both criminals are in jail, but who is to say that other coven members aren't out for revenge?"

"Maybe, but shouldn't we see whether Aunt Fern's boyfriend was who he claimed to be? He might have been the target all along."

My cousin had a point. I didn't know much about him. "I suppose we could look into him, but the biggest hurdle is that no one other than Aunt Fern seems to know him very well."

"I thought his office was in town," Rihanna said.

"It might be, but I don't know where." I looked over at Jaxson. "Can you do a quick search?"

"For a company with the name Upton in it?"

"That's a reasonable start. If you can't find anything, I'll ask Aunt Fern tomorrow. I imagine Steve or Nash will go there and ask questions, and we can't afford to have either of them see us, especially after Steve specifically asked me not to investigate."

"Steve always tells you not to interfere, and yet you—or rather, we—always do."

"True." That was because my magic was needed in the previous cases.

Jaxson stood and headed over to his computer. It took only a minute for him to find something. "Got it. There's a listing for Upton Capital in Witch's Cove. It says here that he is a venture capitalist who provides money for start-ups."

"That matches what Aunt Fern said. I bet Steve could get a warrant to search the Upton Capital records. But even if we find out the company names of those he invested in, where does that leave us?"

"It's Steve's job to speak to each of Peter's clients. No one will admit they were in such a bad way that they had to resort to killing him, so that would be a waste of our time," Jaxson said.

"I agree. And only Steve can look at their bank accounts."

"Maybe Aunt Fern will help," Rihanna said.

"How?"

"I would think she'd know her boyfriend's assistant at least. He or she might have an idea as to who wanted to harm the boss. Someone could have threatened him."

"I agree, but what if his ex-wife lives in town, and she doesn't want anyone snooping?"

"She passed away a few years back," Rihanna said. We looked back at her. "What? I talk to Aunt Fern."

"I'm glad. I'm sure she enjoys your company."

Rihanna sipped her drink. "Do you think Steve would be willing to send us the photos of the attendees?"

I glanced over at Jaxson, but he just shrugged. "Why would he? Steve doesn't want me to investigate unless this case involves magic. Only then he might ask for our help."

"It does involve magic if we go with the idea Peter Upton wasn't the target," Rihanna said. "That Levy or I was."

"Are you saying we should let Steve do the straightforward investigation of Peter Upton, while we look into the coven?"

She shrugged. "I'm pretty sure Levy would be willing to help."

"You both know me. I want to investigate, but going against people who can cloak themselves and move locks with their minds is way out of my league."

"It's not for me," Rihanna stated.

I didn't like where this was headed. "Oh, no, you don't. You are going to finish high school before you entertain any thoughts of being an investigator."

"Seriously?"

Sure, she'd helped solve our last two cases, but I didn't want her to be in harm's way again. "Yes, seriously."

"Ladies." Jaxson held up his hands. "How about we get together with Penny and Hunter, and maybe even Levy? Together, we should be able to figure out who they were really after and who might have worn a Spiderman costume—assuming Dolly is right."

"Dolly is always right—or at least between her and the gossip queens, she is. Someone must have paid attention to who was dressed as what."

"When you and I were taking the money, one guy showed up as Spiderman," Jaxson said.

"You're right. I think he was in line with two other guys, just in front of Rihanna and Gavin."

Rihanna nodded. "I only saw them go into the party. I was behind Raggedy Ann and Andy."

"I must have gotten confused."

"Next year," Jaxson said, "we should outlaw wearing masks—at least upon entering the party."

Like that would ever happen. "We'll talk about it then."

"I have an idea," Rihanna said.

"Yes?"

She grabbed a cookie and took a bite. "What if we talk to Gertrude?"

Rihanna had been training with the powerful witch for the last month. Because of Rihanna's natural proclivity to read minds, Gertrude suggested that her grandson, Levy, help hone her skills. Other than trying to contact the dead though, I wasn't sure what Gertrude was teaching her. Rihanna had been rather tight-lipped about it. "About what?"

She huffed. "About our future."

I must be dense, because I wasn't following. "I don't think that is what Gertrude does. She's a psychic, not a fortuneteller. Even if she were one, do you think she'll tell us that the killer meant to murder Mr. Upton, and that you and Gavin will live happily ever after?"

"I don't know, but she might know if I'm in danger or not."

As much as I believed in Gertrude Poole's abilities, even she would admit that her ability to analyze what she saw in her mind wasn't always accurate. What if Rihanna let down her guard because Gertrude didn't interpret a sign correctly and then was killed? I'd never forgive myself.

"Let's contact Levy tomorrow and see what he has to say. Since he can read minds, maybe he was standing close to the killer right before he did the deed. Something would have gone through the guy's head."

"It's a long shot," my cousin said. "Levy only hears bits and pieces. He might not put the pieces together in the right order."

"But you can?"

"Sometimes, yes. Sometimes, no."

The last thing I wanted was to get into an argument with my cousin. I yawned, even though I wasn't all that sleepy. We were all distraught over what had happened and probably not in the best frame of mind to make any important decisions. "I'm going to head back."

Jaxson stood. "I'll walk you there, but then I'm sleeping here tonight." He held up a hand. "It's just a precaution."

"I'm staying, too," Iggy announced.

"Rihanna will be safe with Jaxson here. Besides, I don't want to be alone tonight." I grabbed my purse and opened it up. "Hop in."

Iggy came over and crawled in, albeit rather reluctantly. "Jaxson won't be long. Lock the door, please." Rihanna was smart enough to do that, but I couldn't stop myself from reminding her.

"Sure, but take your time. I need to shower."

I could understand the need. With Iggy in tow, we left. Once we reached the bottom of the steps, Jaxson stopped and studied the area.

I grabbed his arm. "Are you thinking these men might still be here?"

"One can't be too careful," he said.

"I'm no mind reader, but I can tell you're worried about Rihanna."

"Of course, I'm worried. She's eighteen. I know how crazy I was at that age. No telling if she'll decide to look around and check things out for herself."

My stomach churned. "Tonight?"

"Tonight, tomorrow. Who knows? It's why I want to spend the night at the office. Maybe tomorrow morning, you can stop over at my place and pick up a few things for me. It's not that I can't leave her alone, but I'd like the option of not having to."

"Sure. I'd be happy to."

While I had been to his place one time after I'd passed out from cloaking myself for too long, I would feel a little strange going through his things, but for Rihanna's sake, I would do as he asked.

He reached in his pocket and unhooked a key. "Here's my spare. Keep it."

I refused to read anything into this other than his need for me to grab a change of clothes for him and some toiletries. When we reached the back entrance to the Tiki Hut, I unlocked the entrance and ushered him in. I could have suggested Jaxson head on back, but I was in a selfish mood. I needed a long hug.

At the top of the stairs, I lifted Iggy out of my purse and opened the cat door, motioning him to go into the apartment. He looked back at me with disgust. Too bad. I wanted some alone time with Jaxson. Once my familiar was on the other side, I turned to my partner and leaned my head against his chest. "Thank you for being there for me and for Aunt Fern."

He wrapped his arms around me and pulled me close. "Of course. Are you going to be okay?"

I looked up at him. "I will be after a nice soak in the tub, but I worry that Aunt Fern won't be for a long time. She really cared for Peter."

Jaxson brushed a wisp of hair out of my face. "I know. We'll do what we can to help her."

I wasn't sure what we could do exactly, but I appreciated his willingness. I didn't know who leaned in first, but the kiss that followed was sweet and full of promise.

He leaned back. "Call me if you need anything."

"I will."

Once Jaxson left, I went inside. "Iggy, you need to get clean."

"Ugh."

"I thought you liked water."

"Water yes, soap no."

Ah, the life of an iguana. Soap probably dried his skin. "Come on. Maybe I can clean you up without using it."

## Chapter Five

EVEN THOUGH I barely slept a wink last night, I got up early to see if Aunt Fern wanted me to open up for the cleaning staff. Before the horrible incident, the plan had been for a crew to arrive at seven. After picking up the party trash, they were to wash the floors and then set up the tables and chairs that their company had stored.

"I need to do some running around," I told Iggy, who was still on his stool with his eyes closed.

"I'm sleeping," he shot back. "Go away."

I figured he'd say that. Besides, he was perfectly capable of heading the few hundred feet to the office on his own.

"As you wish." As soon as I stepped out of my apartment, noise from the restaurant filtered upstairs, and relief shot through me. The workers were here, which meant that Aunt Fern had been able to pull herself together enough to get dressed and manage the clean-up.

I found her in the middle of the restaurant dressed in jeans and a t-shirt, something I rarely saw her wear. I didn't know if I should be concerned or not. "Aunt Fern?"

She was talking with one of the workers. When she spotted me, she motioned for him to do something near the bar and then came over. "Oh, Glinda," she said before hugging me.

"I am so sorry for your loss." I inwardly groaned at the cliché, but I'd heard it my whole life. It was what I always said. In this case, I meant it. "I'm glad you didn't tell the workers to get near where Peter was...I mean, near the coffin. Steve asked that we not touch anything behind the crime scene tape."

Her half smile seemed forced. "I figured, dear. What are you doing up so early?"

"I wanted to check up on you."

"I'm good. Thank you."

She wasn't good. Her eyes were still red, probably from crying all night. "Do you have any idea who would want to harm Peter?"

Yes, yes, I know, it wasn't my place to ask, but this was my aunt, and I wanted to help her any way I could.

She shook her head. "I've had all night to think about it, and the answer is still no. Peter didn't expect anyone to pay him back. I think I mentioned that he lent money to start-up companies, but what I meant was that he invested in them. In return, he would receive a portion of the profits."

She had told me. "Did he mention which companies he'd invested in?"

"He might have, but most weren't from around here, so I can't recall."

That I didn't know. "Maybe he was killed by mistake."

Her eyes widened. "By mistake?"

I'd mentioned the possibility yesterday also. She must have forgotten. "I just meant that it was dark, and several people wore vampire costumes. You said it yourself. Peter a good man."

"Good men are often murdered."

"I suppose. Let's hope that the sheriff's department finds something. Is there anything I can do?" Aunt Fern was down here most likely to forget, and here I was dredging up bad memories. Way to go, Glinda!

"No, dear, but I'll let you know if I think of anything."

I hugged her again before heading out. I hopped in my car and drove to Jaxson's place. Being there by myself almost seemed like an invasion of his privacy, but he needed his things.

Once inside, I gathered the items on his list and then headed back to the office. And yes, I was tempted to snoop, but I didn't. I'd even considered making his bed and straightening up a bit, but that would be overstepping anyone's bounds.

When I returned to the office, I was surprised to find that Jaxson and Rihanna were up. "Hey."

I didn't ask if either had slept, as I assumed the answer would be no. My stomach, however, was quite awake if the grumbling coming from it was any indication.

"Hungry?" Jaxson asked with a hint of a smile.

"I am." I handed him the items he'd asked me to pick up.

"Thank you."

"How about we see Dolly?" Rihanna asked.

"Why?" It was too early to be thinking straight.

"We want to eat, and Dolly might have learned something since last night."

If anyone could get to the bottom of this, it would be her. "The Tiki Hut is not open yet, so the Spellbound Diner it is!"

"Where's Iggy?" Jaxson asked.

"He wanted to sleep in."

Jaxson nodded. "Give me five minutes to clean up."

"Sure."

He disappeared into the bathroom. "Did you and Jaxson figure anything out after I left?" I asked.

"Not really. Either Mr. Upton was the target, or he wasn't. Could either Levy or I have been the intended target? Maybe."

I had been worried finding answers would be hard. "This is why we need to ask Dolly."

"I agree."

True to his word, Jaxson emerged from the bathroom in no time. "I'm ready," he stated.

We hadn't reached the bottom steps when who should appear but our sleepy iguana. "Nice of you to join us," I said.

"Where are you going?"

"To the diner."

Without me asking if he wanted to come, he crawled up my leg to my shoulder. Prancing in with Iggy when the town was full of tourists might not be such a good idea, but fortunately I had on a lightweight sweater. Wanting to keep Dolly's goodwill, I placed him underneath.

Inside, the place was packed. That came as no surprise as it was a Sunday morning. Our luck, a couple left their booth, and we snagged it. Dolly was working in the kitchen, but I didn't want to disturb her—at least not yet. Food first and then gossip.

After the server cleared off the table, she took our order. This time, I remembered to ask for the plate of lettuce for

Iggy.

"I'm thinking of seeing if Gertrude can set up a séance," Rihanna said.

"In order to talk to Peter?" I asked.

"Yes. He might have some ideas as to what happened."

"My mom says it often takes days before the deceased is willing to talk."

"Sure, but isn't that because they want some kind of justice first?" she asked.

I was no expert in talking to those who'd passed on, except for the few ghosts who'd come my way. Even then, only one person who hadn't been in his ghost form had spoken directly to me. "I don't know."

"Come on, Glinda. What do we have to lose?" Jaxson's brow rose.

"Nothing. I'm game." I held up a finger. "By the way, I spoke to Aunt Fern this morning."

"How is she?" he asked.

"As good as can be expected." I detailed our discussion about the fact that while Peter invested in growing companies, most were not from around here.

"That's makes researching his firm more difficult."

"Steve will be at a dead end, too, I bet, which is all the more reason to follow the psychic trail. He won't have much access to that," I said.

"He knows Levy," Rihanna said.

"True, but I doubt your mentor would invite the sheriff's department to a coven meeting." Not that he'd ever suggested we go, either.

"What are you thinking?" Jaxson asked.

I had no clear path of attack. "I know Rihanna wants to consult a fortuneteller, but I think talking with Gertrude, who is our most competent psychic, will be our best use of our time. I can ask Mom to join us for the séance if need be since the four of us contacted my Nana the last time."

"What about Jaxson?" Rihanna said. "He should join us."

"I have no problem with the five of us, but Jaxson, are you comfortable with it?"

He inhaled and then pressed his lips together. Before he could answer, our food arrived. I took his delayed response as a probable no. I was going to ask the server to tell Dolly we were here, but when the owner emerged from the kitchen, I'd flag her down. This diner was still a madhouse.

"Come on, Jaxson," Rihanna urged. "It will be fun."

Iggy crawled on my lap. "I'll do it."

I almost laughed, but then thought better of it. He could see and talk to ghosts. Perhaps he had some supernatural powers I was unaware of. "If Gertrude is amenable, we can give it a try," I told him.

He ran up my chest and licked my face. That act of affection took me by surprise since Iggy didn't bestow kisses often.

"I don't think six is a good number," Jaxson said, clearly fighting a smile.

"Next time."

He smiled. "Sure."

We dug into our meal. Halfway through, Dolly came over. "I thought I saw you guys come in. How is Fern? I tried calling, but she didn't answer."

"My aunt is managing the clean-up. She claims she's fine, but she's not really."

"It's such a shame. She and Peter only stopped in here one time, but I got to see them at the art showing. He seemed nice."

"I thought so, too." Even though Dolly seemed anxious to discuss Aunt Fern's mental state, I needed her to answer some questions. "What exactly did you see last night?" I asked.

"Just what I told Steve. No one notices a bag lady, so I was free to wander. In fact, I was heading over to chat with Nash, or at least who I thought was Nash, because I wanted to ask about Pearl, but before I reached him, the man left and joined your aunt. When he kissed her, I realized that vampire had not been our deputy."

"Oh, my," Rihanna said.

"What is it?"

"I spoke to Steve briefly. He asked me about how my work with Gertrude was coming. I told him good, and then I went in search of Gavin, who was getting us some sodas."

"Are you thinking the killer thought you or Peter might have been Nash, because both of you were talking to Steve?"

"I don't know what to think," she said.

Having four lookalikes could be confusing. "Dolly, did you ever find Nash?"

"I did. Like I said, I wanted to chat with him instead of Steve, because I didn't want to bother the sheriff. He and Misty seemed quite cozy, if you get my drift." She winked.

"I'm glad. He needs some balance in his life." Before I'd met Jaxson, I might not have been as pleased. Now? I had no interest in the man.

"Did you see anyone else in a vampire outfit?" I asked.

"One more guy, that's all."

That would have been Levy. "You said you saw a person in a Spiderman costume stab, if that's the right word, the vampire. Right?"

"I saw Spiderman walk up to the vampire, and he was carrying the hook from Steve's Captain Hook outfit. I never saw the actual stabbing, because the lights went out. I did hear someone groan."

That might have been the same groan I heard.

"One more thing. Did you see any other people dressed as Spiderman?" I asked.

"Yes, but I couldn't tell you how many. Pearl said there had only been one—according to Steve. I told her that wasn't right since I distinctly remember several wearing that costume."

Iggy clawed my leg, and I looked down at him. "Tell her about the three men stashing their Spiderman costumes in their car."

I wish I could communicate telepathically with him right now so I could tell him I wasn't comfortable with Dolly knowing about the other men. "I remember only one for sure during the time Jaxson and I manned the front door. Others could have entered through the back entrance, though."

Hopefully, later today, we would get together with Penny, Hunter, and possibly Levy. Between all of us, we should be able to figure out how many had worn Spiderman costumes and why only one appeared after the murder.

Someone called Dolly's name. "I've got to go. Keep me in the loop."

I just waved, not wanting to commit to anything. "Thank you."

She hustled off. "What do we make of this new information?" I asked my crime solving companions.

"Why didn't you tell her about the three men?" Iggy asked.

"I don't want to put her in any more danger. She already saw the killer—or rather kind of saw him. I just hope he doesn't know that Dolly was the bag lady."

"I doubt it," Jaxson said. "Even we couldn't tell with all that makeup."

"Maybe Gertrude can get a handle on this mess," Rihanna said.

"That would be nice. I just wish the killer had left something behind so that Gertrude—or you—could touch it and maybe see something."

"Who's to say he didn't?" Rihanna asked.

"He might have. The cleaning crew could have picked up something. Even Dr. Sanchez might have found a trace."

Once we finished our meal, I paid, anxious to find some answers.

"Can we stop over at the Psychics Corner to see when Gertrude can fit us in?" Rihanna asked.

"We can do that." I turned to Jaxson. "You don't have to come if you don't want to."

"I've changed my mind. If I'm going to be part of some paranormal cult or coven or whatever you call yourselves, I need to learn everything I can."

I loved his new attitude. "Works for me."

We headed over to the Psychics Corner to find Gertrude. Because this was a tourist town, they were open on Sunday, and it being Halloween week, the town was more full than usual. I was convinced parents bused their kids in from neighboring towns to see all of the decorations. I wouldn't be surprised if they told their children they might see some real magic.

Gertrude wasn't in, but the receptionist, who wasn't Sarah this time, said she'd call her, claiming Gertrude never seemed to mind being interrupted despite her advanced age. Because time—and possibly another person's life was on the line—I didn't feel bad asking the receptionist to make the call.

After she contacted her, the receptionist disconnected and smiled. "She'll be here soon."

I never knew where Gertrude lived, but considering she arrived in less than fifteen minutes, I bet it wasn't all that far.

Gertrude entered the large entranceway and smiled. "Isn't this a nice surprise. Are we trying to find out who killed your aunt's boyfriend?"

Now how did she know that?

# Chapter Six

"TELL ME WHAT you know," Gertrude said once we were all seated in her office.

Iggy climbed up on Gertrude's lap, and she seemed quite happy to have him there. I described the Halloween party, who some of the guests were, and then how the lights went out. "Right after Jaxson turned them on, I heard Aunt Fern cry out."

"That's when she saw her dead boyfriend," Gertrude said in a low, faraway sounding voice.

What I wouldn't give to know how Gertrude always knew things. "Yes. Everything was bizarre."

"Bizarre?" Gertrude asked.

I explained how I had placed a mannequin of a vampire in the coffin. "How ironic was it that Peter had on in the same costume, lying on top of my mannequin? To make matters worse, your grandson, Rihanna, and Nash Solana all wore identical ones and are approximately the same height."

She wove her fingers together. "I didn't know Levy was there. hat does confuse things. And you want to know if the person who killed Peter might have been trying to kill someone else." It was a statement rather than a question.

"Yes."

"I don't know."

That answer surprised me.

"Can't you do some psychic spell or something to find out?"

She smiled. "It doesn't quite work that way."

While she was nice about it, I still felt like an ignorant witch.

"How about we conduct a séance so Peter can provide us with answers?" Rihanna asked.

Gertrude pressed her lips together. "That would be wonderful if he would talk to us."

I leaned forward. "You don't sound hopeful."

She held up her hands. "No two séances are the same. I've been working with Rihanna on them, but she can attest that they don't always go as planned."

"That's true," Rihanna said. "I've been trying to reach my dad, but he's been rather stubborn about appearing."

I know that failure had pained her. The last séance we'd done here had my grandmother appearing in her ghost form instead of talking through one of the people at the table. "I'm game if the rest of you are."

Everyone nodded. I was happy that Jaxson didn't make some excuse to leave.

Gertrude pointed to the table in the corner. "Jaxson, if you could pull that table over here, we can get started."

Rihanna stood. "I'll get the candelabra."

Gertrude asked me to close the drapes, saying the dead didn't like a lot of light. "Iggy asked if he could participate. I hope that won't be a problem."

Gertrude looked down at my familiar. "I'm sure his energy will be welcome."

Oh, boy. Now, I'd never hear the end of how amazing he was. I'm sure he was the first iguana in history to take part in a séance. I placed Iggy on the table between me and Rihanna. Jaxson sat down between me and Gertrude.

Our host dimmed the overhead lights using the remote. "We are here to connect to Peter Upton who was taken suddenly and brutally from us. Place your fingertips to the person or animal next to you, and then close your eyes while you open your mind."

It was a bit tricky to do that with Iggy, but we managed.

"Peter, if you can hear us, please help us bring justice to this tragedy. Tell us what you can," Gertrude incanted.

The candles flickered, or at least they seemed to twinkle through my closed eyelids. Whoa. The table just moved. Okay, that could have been my imagination, but it sure seemed real.

"Thank you for trying to help me," said a very deep voice that came from across the table. The strength of the voice implied it wasn't Gertrude pretending to be him, but the real Peter Upton.

My pulse soared. I wanted to open my eyes and see if Gertrude's lips were moving, but I didn't want to chance ruining the spell.

When my grandmother's ghost had appeared, I could talk to her, but I wasn't sure if I could with Peter.

"Do you know who killed you?" Rihanna blurted.

Bless her heart.

"No, but I felt a presence behind me right before someone grabbed my shoulder. Before I could turn around, this sharp pain stabbed me in the back." The voice wobbled. "He...ah...said that I shouldn't have messed with them."

My palms sweated. "Mess with who? Do you know who he meant by *them*?" Fine. I couldn't help but ask.

"No. I swear. I make people's lives better, not worse."

A loud thump sounded across the table from me, and the air pressure in the room seemed to drop, forcing me to open my eyes. Gertrude's forehead was on the table.

"Gertrude?" I choked out.

Rihanna pushed back her chair and stepped over to her mentor. She placed her hands on Gertrude's shoulders. "Don't worry. This is what happens when she does one of these."

What? Why didn't Rihanna warn us? Gertrude was about ninety-years old. She should have asked Rihanna to lead the session, especially if this happened often. Passing out couldn't be good for Gertrude's heart. However, even if my cousin had taken the lead, who was to say Peter wouldn't have spoken through Gertrude anyway?

Gertrude sat up. "What happened?"

She honestly didn't seem to know. "Peter talked through you." I wasn't sure if that was the right term.

"Good. Did he say anything of value?"

I looked at Jaxson, Rihanna, and Iggy. I assumed we all heard the same thing, but I'd like confirmation. "Jaxson, why don't you tell us what you heard."

"I'll get Gertrude some tea," Rihanna said.

"Just that the person who stabbed Peter seemed to be there for revenge. Apparently, he believed Peter had messed with *them*, whoever *them* is."

"Right," I chimed in. "Only Peter said he never messed

with anyone. He doesn't know what the man was referring to."

"Or he isn't admitting it," Rihanna said as she handed Gertrude her drink.

I shook my head. "Peter is dead. It's not like he can be arrested for a crime now. No, I don't think he was the intended target."

My cousin sat back down. "We're back to the idea again that Spiderman meant to kill me or Levy?"

"Or Nash," I added.

Gertrude sucked in a breath. "If I may speak as a non-psychic for a moment, you and Levy did interfere with one of Levy's coven members."

"Enough for them to want to kill either one, just because we caught some guy in the act of robbing a house?" I asked.

"I don't know, but possibly. Putting back on my psychic's hat, I'll need more information."

"What kind of information?" I asked.

"Perhaps something that belonged to the killer. I realize that's a tall order, but if you have a suspect, perhaps you can bring me an item he's touched."

"We'll try. Or maybe Levy can help," I said.

"Maybe." Gertrude didn't sound happy about that.

"We need to meet with him tonight," Jaxson said. "We can't afford to wait too long. The killer might learn that they murdered the wrong person and return."

"He probably knows. It's been on social media already." Rihanna held up her hand. "And not by me."

Social media. Just what we didn't need. Thank goodness Aunt Fern wasn't into that kind of thing.

Gertrude nodded. "Okay. I'll call and ask him. I'm sure he'll want to help."

We discussed possible times. After Gertrude contacted him, he agreed to come over at seven since he had a meeting to run first. Whether he could add anything to this bizarre crime, I had no idea.

By dinnertime, the Tiki Hut was open for business, but since Aunt Fern wasn't manning the cash register, I assumed she was resting. I had gone over there to order our evening meeting snacks for the six of us: me, Jaxson, Rihanna, Levy, Penny, and Hunter.

Between us, we should be able to figure out what happened last night. I suppose we could have invited Nash since he'd worn a vampire costume, but I didn't want him asking us to stay out of the investigation. This was too important to stop now.

I debated telling Steve what our victim told us about the murder being an act of revenge, and while he might—and that was a big might—believe us, he'd just say there was nothing he could do with that additional information. His job as an officer of the law was to investigate why someone would want to murder a wealthy venture capitalist.

In truth, I was happy he was working that angle. There was no way Jaxson and I could have looked into all of the leads without the ability to get a search warrant.

After I paid for the food, I rushed back to the office. No sooner had I set out the snacks than Penny and Hunter showed up.

I hugged my friend first and then Hunter. "Thanks for coming."

"I wish it was under better circumstances, but tonight is a good night. Tommy is with his father."

"Good timing for me, too," Hunter said. "After the wolf attacks a few months back, the county gave me an assistant who will be staying late tonight."

"That's great. You can use the help." Those wolf attacks weren't from real wolves but rather from werewolves. "Does your new assistant know what he's up against?"

Hunter smiled. "Why, yes *she* does."

My eyes widened. "A she?"

He chuckled. "Yes. I told them I had a great person for the job. Heather Langley is from our clan in Montana."

"Your clan? She's a werewolf?" Rihanna asked. Her eyes sparkled, but her open mouth implied she was shocked and maybe not all that happy.

Hunter looked over at me. "You didn't tell her?"

She hadn't been ready—or maybe I was the one who wasn't ready to tell her. "Not yet."

"I'm not ready?" Rihanna asked. "Were you going to wait until I'd turned twenty-one before telling me? Don't you think you should have said something before now?"

I could feel the ground sinking beneath me.

Jaxson stepped up next to me and then turned to Hunter and Penny. "I guess Glinda forgot to mention that Rihanna can kind of read minds."

"My bad. I think you mentioned that, but I forgot," Penny said.

"I'm cool with werewolves and all," Rihanna said. "I mean, if I can handle people being able to disappear and moving locks with their minds, I can deal with a person changing into a wolf, I guess."

My cousin was a trooper. When Hunter didn't say anything, I felt the need to move this conversation along. "Please have a seat. Our resident warlock should be here soon."

Both Penny and Hunter were well aware of how Levy had helped in the last case. Everyone grabbed a drink and some chips.

"Do you have any leads?" Hunter asked.

"Yes and no." I told them about the séance. I probably should have waited until Levy arrived, but if he had a meeting, he might be running late.

"If you believe Peter never attacked anyone, then he wasn't the target," Hunter said.

A knock sounded, and Levy came in. "Sorry, I'm late."

Jaxson, Rihanna, and I were pressed together on the couch, while Penny and Hunter sat in chairs across from us. Iggy was wandering around somewhere. I was sure he'd put in his two cents when he had something to offer.

"No problem. I was getting Penny and Hunter caught up about the séance your grandmother held for us this morning."

"She told me what Peter Upton claimed. But that still begs the question whether *them*—the term the killer had used—referred to Steward Winthrop's coven or not." He sat in the remaining chair.

"If we're opening up this discussion to clans, he could have been referring to Nash's clan." Hunter glanced over at me.

"Neither of them knows about our deputy either," I said, referring to Rihanna and Levy who never had the need to be told anything about werewolves. Rihanna had been working to get over the death of her father, and I figured a teenager could only deal with so much at once.

Her eyes widened. "Really? Nash is a werewolf, too?" Her mouth opened slightly as she swiveled her head to Hunter. "I guess it makes sense." She looked at Levy, probably daring him to read her mind.

"Hunter and Nash are werewolves?" He laughed, but no one joined in.

"I could demonstrate, but I have no desire to end up naked in front of our impressionable teenager," Hunter said.

I didn't want that either, but this time I didn't voice my opinion.

Levy held up his hand. "That's okay. I believe you. That does open up a whole new path of issues. If the killer meant to take out Nash, I'm assuming you can't tell who's a werewolf and who isn't?"

"*We* absolutely can tell who is and who isn't. That is what has me thinking our kind wasn't being targeted. I don't think the killer is one either. I would have sensed him."

"If the killer was targeting Nash, he'd have to have been a werewolf, right?" Levy asked.

I held up my hand, almost as if I was back at school. "Maybe this has nothing to do with any clan business. Hunter, you worked with Nash back in Montana. Maybe he arrested someone from a group of thieves or drug dealers or something, and this person wants to get back at him for that. This person might not even be aware of your kind."

Hunter cocked a brow. "It is possible, but would someone

come all the way from Montana to exact revenge?"

"I don't see why not. If the killer isn't from around here, he could leave without much notice."

Levy nodded. "She has a point."

"We'll need to mention that to Steve tomorrow," Jaxson suggested. "In order to speed things up, I will offer my time to research some of the one hundred people at the party."

"That's a great idea," I said.

"Guys, we may be looking at this all wrong. Maybe the killer hired a witch to do a spell that prevented him from sensing another werewolf and vice versa," Rihanna said. "Gertrude has been teaching me about love potions—and no, I'm not going to use one on Gavin. She said that the sense of smell is very powerful."

I could see where she was going with this. "That's brilliant," I said. "The killer could be a werewolf. He could have requested a spell be put on him so that Nash, Hunter, my dad, or any werewolf couldn't identify him. The downside would be that he wouldn't know they were one either."

"Hold on," Rihanna said. "Uncle Stan is a werewolf?"

"Yes. Long story. I'll fill you in later."

She twisted toward Jaxson. "Are you one, too?"

He chuckled. "I might be Superman, but I'm no werewolf."

For that, I was glad. "Rihanna has a point though. We have to consider the killer is a werewolf. Then again, it's also possible he isn't one."

"Great," Jaxson said. "We can't even decide if Peter Upton was the target or not."

"I'm not so sure," Levy said.

"What do you mean?"

## Chapter Seven

"FOR THE RECORD, let me say that I don't know much about werewolf physiology," Levy admitted.

"Anything you'd like to know, feel free to ask," Hunter said.

"I appreciate that. You can normally sense another wolf, right?"

"Yes."

"Maybe this killer is a warlock—or a witch—who is also a werewolf," Levy said.

My blood almost turned cold. "That combination would be sincerely deadly."

"Exactly," Levy said. "Not all warlocks can cloak themselves with an incantation or open locks in seconds. I'm guessing the same might be true for werewolves."

"You're implying only a special kind of werewolf can cloak his scent like a warlock can cloak his body?"

"Precisely."

We sat there in silence for a few seconds, trying to absorb that new concept. "Let me make sure I understand all this cloaking stuff," Jaxson said. "You're saying that the killer might be a werewolf who can disguise his scent, which possibly prevents him from scenting any other werewolf. To the general public, he's an ordinary human."

Levy nodded. "Yes."

"In that case, he could have been targeting Nash because of some transgression he's done either in Witch's Cove or in Montana," Jaxson added.

"That would be my guess."

I never could stop my mind from looking at alternatives. "On the other hand, the killer could be a regular human who was targeting Peter. If not Peter, then maybe he was interested in Rihanna or you, Levy." I chugged the rest of my drink that I wished had been a glass of wine. "All that boils down to is that we have squat."

"Not completely," Penny said. She'd been rather quiet up until now.

"What are you thinking?" I asked.

"I know that Hunter and I let in one Spiderman during the time we were taking money."

"And I know for a fact that Jaxson and I took in one. That makes two."

Iggy crawled out from under the sofa. "I saw three."

All but Hunter could hear him, so I told Hunter what my familiar said and what he'd seen after the lights went out.

"I'll play the devil's advocate here," Hunter said. "Suppose we let in three Spidermen who might or might not have been working together. One of them killed Peter who may or may not have been the target. In case anyone saw him, he could say it wasn't him but rather one of the other Spidermen."

It was logical. "Why change their outfits after the kill? Why not just leave?" I asked.

"Easy. Leaving would have made them persons of interest," Hunter said.

My shoulders slumped. "All this means is that we have endless possibilities. Or am I wrong?"

"You're not wrong," Jaxson said.

"We could sit here for a few more hours and debate whether the killer was a werewolf and who he might be after, but I don't think we'd reach any consensus," Hunter said.

Levy slapped his thighs. "I agree. I'll ask some of my coven members to see if they've heard any rumblings about a group wanting revenge for us putting Winthrop and his partner, Phil Dimitri, in jail."

"Good idea."

Hunter waved his hand. "I'll talk to Nash to see if we can come up with some groups who might want to target him. Nash spent years in Montana arresting people. For much of the time though, he and I went after the clan members who didn't treat ordinary humans with respect."

Penny placed a hand on Hunter's arm. "Does that mean you could be in danger?"

"I'll be fine."

I doubt that answer would satisfy Penny for long. I inhaled deeply and then blew out a long breath. "Okay. I'll email everyone so we can stay connected. If you learn anything, please share."

We chatted a bit more, and then everyone left. My mind was exhausted, as was my body. Not sleeping last night was catching up to me. I couldn't help but yawn—for real this time.

"Let me walk you home," Jaxson said.

"Thanks."

After collecting Iggy, we left. This time I didn't need to warn Rihanna to lock up after us since she seemed sufficiently afraid not to take any chances.

"What's your main takeaway from our group meeting?" Jaxson asked once we were away from the office.

"Whoever killed Peter was smart. The murder seemed planned—other than possibly killing the wrong person."

"That's smart?" he asked.

"How many people can kill someone then hide in plain sight and not get caught?"

"Probably not many. If he was part warlock, he might be able to cloak himself."

"That's an even scarier thought." I shivered. "I really, really want this guy, whether he's a werewolf, warlock, or human." I looked up at Jaxson. "The worst part is that we have too many suspects and no clues."

He rubbed my back. "We'll get some."

"How?"

"Glinda, don't worry. Steve and Misty are on the case. Something will come our way."

"I hope you are right."

TO MY SURPRISE, I actually slept last night, but that was only after an hour of trying to figure things out. I failed, of course, mostly because I couldn't reconcile what Iggy saw with what might have happened. I believed there were at least four Spidermen who came to the party yet only one left as one. It was as if those three men that Iggy saw, whoever they were,

were involved somehow.

Something clawed on my arm. It was Iggy. "Go away."

I was still in bed, wanting the chance to think things through for another few minutes.

"It's after ten. We have a crime to solve. I'm heading over to the office," Iggy said.

Ten? I bolted upright. I never slept in that late. "Tell Jaxson I'm on my way."

I was out of bed and dressed in less than fifteen minutes, which just might be a new record for me. When I exited my apartment, noise rose from downstairs meaning the restaurant was open for business. Whether Aunt Fern was running things, or her substitute cashier, Bertie Stillwell was, I didn't know. I feared that if I checked in, Aunt Fern would ask me to stay and do something. As much as I wanted to help, my time would be better spent if I worked on solving this crime.

Focused on doing just that, I slipped out the side entrance and nearly tripped on a garbage bag. "Really?"

Had Rihanna left it there? Or had the clean-up crew forgotten to put it in the dumpster? Ugh. Hating any kind of trash, I grabbed the bag to dispose of it when I happened to glance down at the ground. I halted. A red glove that had a blue and white spider pattern on it was crushed against the wall. My mind raced. Had this belonged to the killer? Iggy saw the men dump their costumes in their truck, so how was this left behind? I had to assume it was dropped by mistake.

It didn't matter how it got there. This might be evidence. Using only my nails, I lifted it up. Steve would need this. In case the bag didn't contain trash from the party, I set it inside. I'd check it out later.

When I entered the sheriff's office, I dangled the glove in

front of Pearl. "Can you get me an evidence bag?"

"Oh, my. What is it?"

I thought she'd figure it out. "It's a glove that came from a Spiderman outfit."

Pearl's eyes widened. "Did the killer drop that?"

I was glad she could put the pieces together. "I don't know." I looked over her shoulder. "Is Nash or Steve here?"

"Nash is with Hunter Ashwell, but Steve is here." She called him.

A moment later the sheriff appeared with an evidence bag. "Where did you find this?" he asked as he opened the bag. I dropped it in.

"Next to the outside door to the Tiki Hut that runs along the alleyway."

He glanced at his grandmother and then back at me. "Come into my office."

I wasn't sure what more I could tell him, but I'd share what I could. On the way, I texted Jaxson to say I found a clue and was now with Steve. I would have been more specific, but it would have been rude to text once in his office.

"I know I asked you not to get involved, but I've learned that no matter what I say, you never listen. So, what have you figured out?"

He wasn't mad then? Interesting tidbit. Since I wanted to make certain Nash was aware that he might have been the target, I discussed what the group of us did or didn't figure out. I was curious to hear Steve's reaction.

"Let me get this straight. This killer might be a werewolf or possibly a warlock who was able to block his ability to be noticed, or he might have been a human who meant to harm Peter Upton. Either that, or he goofed and was really after

Nash because my deputy arrested someone this killer cared about?"

"That about sums it up."

"And the glove? What do you make of that?"

I told him what Iggy saw. "It's possible these men took off their Spiderman costumes in the side alley and then dressed in other costumes before returning."

"I thought you said they were wearing street clothes when they were at their car."

I had to think about that. "I did say that, but come to think of it, I don't believe Iggy claimed one way or the other. I might have assumed it."

"Just so you know, no one came back in street clothes."

"That means they might have changed somewhere." I found that odd.

"Did your iguana tell you the make and model of the car where they stashed their costumes?" I couldn't tell if he was being sarcastic or sincere, but I'd answer him, nonetheless.

"No, and I doubt he'd know. Iggy isn't a car person. Besides, it would have been too dark to tell a color, but I will ask him."

"Good. And this trash bag you found. What was in it?"

"My hands were full at the time so I couldn't look inside. Not wanting anyone else to pick it up, I put it inside the restaurant. When I get back, I'll check."

"You do that. In the meantime, I'm going to make sure that no one wanted Peter Upton dead before moving on to another conspiracy theory."

"Just because I have no proof doesn't make it a conspiracy theory. Levy Poole thinks it's possible. In fact, he's talking to his coven members to see if they have heard any gossip. Do you have any tangible proof that Peter was the target?"

"No."

There you go. "My goal is to make sure this guy doesn't harm Rihanna or Levy."

"I'm sorry if I came off as being insensitive. I do think you might be on the right track. It's why Nash is with Hunter. They are trying to figure out if someone from their past is after them."

My heartbeat soared. "That's great. What about the photos? Did they recognize anyone?"

"No," Steve said. "That doesn't mean someone from their past wasn't involved, however. Their clan in Montana could have hired some thugs to carry out their revenge."

That made sense. "Jaxson said he'd be happy to help anyway he could. The man is a wizard when it comes to computer searches."

"I appreciate that, but I gave half of the list of names that I didn't recognize to Misty to see what she could come up with. I have a feeling this guy doesn't have a record though."

"Which means he won't be in the system."

"Correct."

"You might want to show Levy the photos of the partygoers. He might recognize an angry coven member."

"I'll consider doing that," Steve said.

I'd done my civic duty for the day. "I'll check out the trash bag. If it contains three sets of street clothes, I'll let you know."

He smiled. "I appreciate it."

Turning over the glove had been the right thing to do, but Gertrude or Rihanna might have gotten a reading off of it. I worried that after the lab processed it, the essence of the person might be gone. Regardless, I would ask to borrow it and see what our resident psychics had to say about it.

I returned to the Tiki Hut, anxious to check out what was in the garbage bag. When I opened it, my nose told me right away that someone had dumped their trash in the alley. Not wanting it in the hallway, I tossed it. To say I was disappointed would be an understatement.

I hadn't been gone more than half an hour, but in that time, I hoped Jaxson had learned something. I raced up the office staircase and found Hunter inside. That was a surprise.

"Hi. I thought you were with Nash."

"I was. How did you hear about that?"

I told him and Jaxson about the glove and how I'd turned it in to Steve. "It was definitely a Spiderman glove." I looked around. "Where's Iggy?"

He popped out from under the sofa. "Here I am."

"The sheriff was very interested in your sighting of the three men, Iggy."

Naturally, he puffed out his chest. "Yes?"

"Do remember what they were wearing?" I asked him.

His eyes faced away from me. "No."

He was no help. "Could they have been wearing other costumes or were they in street clothes?"

"It was dark."

That was his way of saying he had been focused on what they'd tossed in the car and not on what they had on. "That's okay."

"Glinda, Hunter has some news."

I hadn't been thinking. Hunter wouldn't be here if something hadn't happened. "What is it?" I sat down across from him.

## *Chapter Eight*

"WE FOUND A man mauled to death in the woods," Hunter said.

My mind splintered at the word *mauled* and what that might mean. "Another murder? How horrible. Was he a werewolf?"

"I don't know. He was in his human form when we found him. Considering he wasn't wearing any clothes, I suspect he was one."

"Are you saying that when a werewolf dies, he turns back into his human form?" Since my dad was a werewolf, I should know—only I didn't.

"Yes."

Jaxson leaned forward. "Did you know this man?"

"His face was so severely damaged that it was impossible to tell if we did or didn't know him."

Ouch. "Are you thinking the destruction of his face was done on purpose?" I asked.

"That was our guess. When a werewolf goes for the kill, he tries to rip out the heart. Harming the face would be an afterthought. I imagine the medical examiner will be able to determine if the defacing was post mortem or not."

I shivered at that thought. "Could this man have been

someone who attended the Halloween party?"

"Nash is working on that angle, but it's not like he can compare this man's face to the photos they took."

What kind of person would do that to another human being? "Have there been a lot of werewolf killings around here that we haven't heard about?" That would be scary if it were true.

"Werewolf killings are rare. The last time was that fellow from our bowling league. What was his name?"

"Diamond Dirk Draper."

Hunter pointed a finger at me. "That's the one."

"Do you have any idea who might have killed the new man?" Jaxson asked.

"No. All we know is that he was killed by two werewolves," Hunter said.

"How could you tell?" Jaxson asked.

"Just like no two people have the same fingerprints, each werewolf's claws are different. The marks on this man's chest were different from those on his back."

I grunted. "What a horrible way to die. Who found him?"

"My new assistant was driving around when she spotted some buzzards overhead. That led her to the body."

"Poor woman. I bet she never thought she'd find a dead body during her first week on the job," I said.

"It's not the best way to start, for sure, but Heather is tough. She's no stranger to death."

I glanced over at Jaxson, but he was staring off into space. "Remember that Iggy saw three men from the party together outside after the lights went out," I said. "If—and that's a big assumption—this guy was one of the three werewolves, why would his friends attack him?"

Hunter shrugged. "I think speculating at this point is a waste of our energies. We'll have to see what both Nash and the good doctor come up with. I just stopped over to let you know about this new development."

And not to have some prolonged session of *what if.* I totally understood. "I appreciate you letting us know, but aren't you scared, especially after what just happened?"

"Me, why?"

"You and Nash worked together. Who's to say these men aren't on a killing spree, and you or Nash are next?"

"For starters, Peter wasn't a werewolf, assuming you're implying they are after my kind. Secondly, I don't think two werewolves would go around eliminating every werewolf. That makes no sense. And thirdly, if they are after Nash, that doesn't necessarily involve me."

"How do you know?"

"We didn't cover the same cases, but don't worry, we will be careful. Until we know for sure that the killer meant to take out Peter Upton and not one of us, we all need to be vigilant."

"I totally agree." I held up a finger. "Let me ask you this. If the dead man had been a werewolf, wouldn't you have been able to tell by his scent?"

"Not after he was dead."

"Oh." We were back to step one. That meant Rihanna couldn't let her guard down either. Once Hunter left, I turned to Jaxson. "Your thoughts?"

"Probably the same as yours. We need to wait until Nash learns if this man was at the party." He grunted. "We should have asked Hunter if they found the man's clothes."

"To see if he had any ID on him?" I asked.

"Yes."

"If there had been, Hunter would have told us his name."

Jaxson nodded. "True."

"I think our best chance to learn something will be after Dr. Sanchez cleans up the face. I remember reading somewhere about scans that can compare eye widths and the distance between the nose and the mouth and stuff. If she had access to one of those, Dr. Sanchez could compare it to the photos of the partygoers."

Jaxson chuckled. "If this were a big city maybe, but I doubt Witch's Cove has one."

He was right. Our tiny town couldn't afford such sophisticated equipment. There hadn't been enough murders. "This is turning into a nightmare."

"All the more reason we have to find out who did this. Personally, I'm leaning toward a werewolf being responsible for Upton's death, even though Peter wasn't one," Jaxson said.

"As much as I want to believe that for Rihanna's and Levy's sake, I don't want them to become complacent. Any idea what our next move should be?"

"Let's suppose for the sake of argument that the person who killed Peter meant to kill Nash instead," Jaxson said.

"Fair guess."

"Nash said he couldn't sense any werewolf other than Hunter or your dad."

We'd gone over this last night. "Which meant the guy either had the ability to cloak his scent, because he was part warlock, or he had a witch put a spell on him."

"Exactly," Jaxson said. "Here's my point. If he asked to

have a spell to cloak his scent, maybe there is a spell to undo it."

"That's a great thought, but I have no idea if something like that even exists."

"Which is why we—or rather you—need to investigate," Jaxson said. "It's not like we have a lot of options right now."

That was true. "I can speak to Gertrude."

"Why not Bertha? I thought she was your go-to girl for spells."

"Bertha doesn't know about werewolves. Don't worry, if Gertrude can't help, maybe Levy will have an idea. He's a powerful warlock."

Jaxson smiled. "I say go for it."

His enthusiasm almost made me believe I could do this. Even if a spell existed, there was still one big hurdle to face—that of who to aim the spell at. If these men could cloak their scent, even Hunter or Nash wouldn't know who was or wasn't a werewolf. That little detail wasn't going to stop me from trying, however.

I walked over to the Psychics Corner and asked to see Gertrude, but she was with a client. I didn't mind waiting the half hour since I could use the time to sort things out. I was hoping I'd overlooked some fact that would be the key to unlocking this mystery.

Once Sarah told me it was my time, I rushed down the hallway to Gertrude's office, knocked, and then stepped inside.

"Glinda. Nice to see you. Have a seat."

I figured her grandson had filled her in about our discussion yesterday since he said he would seek her counsel. "Have you ever heard of werewolves being able to cloak their scent?"

"Not before Levy mentioned it."

I told her about the man who'd been murdered.

"I didn't know there had been another death," she said.

I was surprised she hadn't sensed it or something. "Hunter Ashwell and Nash think the dead man was a werewolf."

"That is disturbing, but even if I could locate this spell you asked about, how would you know who to put the spell on?"

"That is the problem."

"I will look for one," Gertrude said, "but for it to work, you'll need to be able to identify these men."

"I know. I found a glove that the killer might have dropped on his way out of the party the other night. I'm hoping that will help."

Gertrude's eyes sparkled. "Now that is something I could use to maybe get some answers."

I explained that it was being processed. "I don't know how long that will take, however."

"When you have it, see if you can bring it to me. I might be able to get an image off of it."

Wouldn't it be nice if she could see in her mind's eye what the killer looked like? "I will do that, and thank you."

"Any time, dear. Does Levy know of this new development?"

"No, I just found out."

"I'll be sure to let him know."

I wished she'd been able to come up with some general spell to expose all werewolves in town, but apparently something like that didn't exist. With a promise from Gertrude that she'd try to help me, I returned to our office.

"Learn anything?" Jaxson asked.

"Not really." I relayed what Gertrude had said. "How about you?"

"Nothing, which means it's now a waiting game for the results and such. I was thinking, since no one has asked for our services of late, I might see if Drake needs me to do some ordering or data entry."

"I can pick up a few shifts at the restaurant, too." Unfortunately, business had been slow of late for Aunt Fern, and she might not need the extra help. What bothered me the most was that we had to keep augmenting our struggling business with an income from other jobs. We had talked about the fact that building a business would take work, but I was losing patience. It didn't help that most crimes went straight to the sheriff's department, but that was how law enforcement worked.

It would be a dream if someday the town council saw fit to give us a monthly stipend to be consultants to the department, but I wasn't going to hold my breath that it would happen any time soon.

"You hungry?" Jaxson asked.

I chuckled. "When am I not?" I hadn't eaten breakfast, but if I mentioned it, he'd say something about me not taking care of myself.

"How about we head on over to the Tiki Hut? We can eat there and keep an eye on your aunt at the same time."

"That sounds great. Plus, if Steve learns anything, I imagine Pearl will pass it on to Aunt Fern."

He tapped his forehead. "That's good thinking."

I smiled. After I gathered Iggy, the three of us went down the street and entered the restaurant. When I looked over at the corner where Peter had been murdered, I was thankful, everything had been cleaned up. Regardless, the reminder was still there, so Jaxson and I grabbed a seat far from the crime scene. I didn't see Penny and had to assume she had the day off.

Aunt Fern rushed over. "This is a nice surprise."

She sounded cheerful enough, but I could still hear the pain in her voice. "We thought we'd see how things are going and ask if Pearl called with any news."

"About what?"

I couldn't tell if she was being coy or not. "I don't know. Was Steve able to narrow down the partygoer list? I know he doesn't believe all one hundred people at the party could be guilty of murder."

"Pearl mentioned that between Steve and Misty, they only identified about half of the people, but that she helped narrow it down by another thirty or so. I think she was going to pass the list to Dolly, Miriam, and Maude. I bet they'll know most of the rest. She did say that the person at the end of the party who was wearing the Spiderman costume was Craig Compton."

"I don't know him."

"He's been away at law school for several years. He just returned home to study for the bar. There is no evidence that he was involved."

"That's good to know, but why didn't Pearl ask you to help go through the names? It was your party."

She leaned closer. "I think they believe it would have been too hard on me—emotionally that is. I swear it wouldn't have. Did I adore Peter? Yes. Did I think we might have had a future? Possibly, but not right away. There were things he never confided in me."

That sounded cryptic. "Like what?"

"Like where did he get his money? Did he inherit it or earn it the old-fashioned way? If so, how? And why did he move to Witch's Cove when he had a very successful business in New York?"

"Maybe he didn't like the cold or the hectic lifestyle." It was why many people moved to Florida. I was surprised she hadn't ever asked him about that.

"Perhaps." She ran a hand over her rather wild hair. Aunt Fern wasn't wearing her usual fairy crown that helped tame her mane, a sure sign she wasn't sleeping well. "The more I think about it, the more I'm convinced Peter might have been the target."

That came out of nowhere. "Why? Because he was mysterious? Did Pearl tell you something?"

"No. It's just a hunch."

Aunt Fern's hunches were usually spot on. The problem was the death of this new man cast Peter's death in a different light. Not that we had any proof her boyfriend's murder was even related to the new man's death, but it was possible that Nash had been the original target—not Peter. For all we know, some crazy werewolf clan up north might have hired these men to do the job of taking Nash out. It was also possible that some crazed warlock coven wanted revenge against either Rihanna or Levy. With the lack of clues, we might never know the truth.

I needed to tell her about the glove I found. That might perk her up. "Don't tell anyone, but I found a glove outside our side entrance door that belonged to someone wearing a Spiderman outfit. I'm hoping that leads us to the identity of the killer." It would be great if they found Peter's blood on the outside and some DNA on the inside. Just my luck, it belonged to this law student kid and not one of the three man that Iggy had seen.

"Oh, that's right. Pearl said you brought it in."

So much for keeping any kind of secret. "I'm assuming Pearl will leak the results to you if the lab comes up with anything."

"I believe so."

"When she does, can you let me know? Gertrude might be able to get a reading off of the glove."

"What kind of reading?"

"She thinks she'll be able to tell what the man who lost it looks like, or whether he is evil or not." That last part, I made up.

"I'll be sure to let you know." She looked over at the counter where a small line was forming. "I need to check them out." She waved to one of the servers. "Enjoy your lunch."

Once she left, I turned to Jaxson. Iggy had crawled out of my purse and had gone somewhere, but I wasn't worried. The Tiki Hut was his home. "What do you make of it? Is Peter still in the running for being the intended target?"

"At this point, I can't commit to anything."

He was a man after my own heart—sometimes indecisive and at other times highly focused.

We ordered and had almost finished when Aunt Fern rushed over with a grin on her face. She handed me a piece of paper. "Pearl came through."

"What is this?"

"I have the names of the three men from the party that no one knows anything about. Steve was able to get their addresses off of their driver's licenses."

That was huge. "Are they from around here?" If so, it might eliminate them from being hired by some werewolf clan in Montana.

"They have Florida driver's licenses."

"Thanks." Darn. That could mean they were local coven members. If they had been from Montana, why get Florida licenses if they only planned to stay a short while? If they only got them to cover their tracks, these men were highly sophisticated and determined.

"What are you going to do?" she asked.

"I'll let Steve question them." I smiled sweetly.

While true, I had my own plan brewing, but I wasn't about to tell my aunt. She'd just tell Pearl who, in turn, would mention it to Steve. At some point, our dear sheriff might decide to lock me up for interfering with an investigation.

# *Chapter Nine*

"I KNOW YOU, Glinda. Tell me what you're thinking," Jaxson said once we were back in the office and out of ear shot of my aunt.

Iggy, who'd had the sense to return just as I was paying, hopped out of my purse. "Spill," he said.

I laughed. "Fine. You know I want to check out these guys."

"Of course I know that, but even you have to realize that one of them could be a killer."

"Yes, and one of them might be dead, implying these men will do anything to get what they want." What that something was, I didn't know.

"But that won't stop you, will it?" he asked.

"No. We have their addresses so maybe we could see where they are living. Why, you might ask? What if they just came down here for the sole purpose of the kill? I would think they'd live near each other and in a rather unassuming place." I held up a finger. "If Peter was the target, they'd be moving on since he is dead."

"It's possible, but don't forget they have their Florida drivers' licenses. That doesn't seem like they plan to leave right away. But that could just be me. On the other hand, if they did arrive recently, Steve would know how long ago from the date on their licenses. I don't have access to that information, and I doubt he'd share."

"I agree. Let's say these guys are renters, since I doubt they would have had time to buy a house. Someone connected around here will know their landlords. Maybe they'll tell us the start date of their leases and if they are good tenants."

"Are you assuming a killer would be a bad tenant? I would think they would be model citizens so as not to attract attention."

Why did Jaxson always poke holes in my theories? "You could be right, but we should at least do a drive by. We don't need to stop. We'll just check out the neighborhood."

Iggy crawled up Jaxson's leg. "Let's do this, boss."

Boss? What was I? While I wanted to know, I didn't have the heart to ask.

"Sure. We might as well. We have no other leads."

I smiled.

I entered the three addresses into my Waze program. "The three houses are fairly close to each other." I was feeling rather smug that I figured they would be. So what if Witch's Cove was a small town?

"That proves nothing," Jaxson said. "If these three men are friends, at least they were smart not to room together—assuming they came here to kill someone."

Once more, I was struck by how many assumptions we had to make, but four possible targets and three possible killers presented a lot of combinations.

"I wonder if their neighbors know where they work. Their bosses might offer some insight," I said.

"Glinda."

I knew that tone. "I wasn't planning to do anything dangerous. I figured the more information we have the better. Maybe our gossip queens would be willing to help."

"How?"

"They might be able to subtly ask around without raising suspicion."

"I like that plan better."

I figured he would. We went out to Jaxson's car. "The first stop is 1134 Herman Avenue." I then gave him the directions.

The area was far from the beach and a bit rundown, but a person could move around unnoticed living there. The first man's home was small and had a chain link fence around the property. No car was in the driveway, but that was to be expected if he was at work. I pressed the video on my phone and panned the neighborhood. "This is where Travis Knowlton lives," I announced.

"Do you want to talk to some neighbors?" Jaxson asked once I'd finished.

"Not today. I don't want any of them to tip off Knowlton, even though I'm sure Nash or Steve have already been here."

Jaxson chuckled. "You just don't want any of the neighbors complaining that some blonde was snooping around."

I twisted toward him. "It's almost scary how well you know me."

He merely grinned. The next two places were low-income apartment complexes. The more I learned about these three men, the more I was convinced they knew each other. I had nothing specific to tie them together, but my gut was working overtime.

"Now what?" he asked.

"I could use a coffee."

"Best idea yet," Jaxson said. "To the Bubbling Cauldron we go."

"Iggy, you can stay in my purse, or do you want me to drop you at home? Your choice," I said.

"I need to hear the scoop."

"Miriam's it is."

Jaxson parked in front of our office, and we walked across the street to the coffee shop. "Are you going to show her the addresses and ask her to investigate?" he asked.

"More or less." I smiled. "If nothing else she might be able to give us the names of people who are either rental agents or who own rental property in that part of town."

"Sounds like a plan."

We went inside and sat near the window since I loved to people watch. A few seconds later, a erver came over and took our order. We'd eaten recently, so I merely ordered a coffee, heavily dosed with cream and sugar, of course. Jaxson went with his usual black sludge. Iggy knew there was nothing here for him, so he didn't ask.

I spotted Miriam in the kitchen and figured once she saw us, she'd come out. I had no problem telling her about the glove and the dead man, since Pearl had probably already filled her in. As for the identity of the three men, Miriam had been involved in vetting the list.

Moments later, she carried out our drinks. "I'm glad to see you two. How is Fern? And I mean how is she really?"

"I'm not sure I know. She claims she's fine, but I can tell she is sad at losing Peter. Aunt Fern really seemed to have cared for him."

"I thought so, too. Did she tell you we were able to narrow the partygoers' list down to only a few suspects?" Thankfully, she kept her voice low.

"Yes. In fact, that's why we're here."

Her eyes lit up, and she pulled out a chair. "How can I help?"

I showed her the list of addresses. I'd taken a photo of the paper in case I needed to give this one to her. "We were wondering if you could point us in the direction of someone who might know who owns these rental properties."

She studied the addresses. "I know of a few people who might be able to help. I'll give them a call right now."

"You are amazing."

Miriam actually blushed. "No promises now."

"Anything will help."

She left and headed to the back. We took our time sipping our coffees, lost in our own thoughts. Before we had finished our first cup, Miriam rushed out.

"This was easier than I thought." She handed us a piece of paper with the name Christina Thompson printed on it, along with her cell number.

"Who is she?"

"A realtor. About a month ago, she rented all three places."

One month? Excitement surged. Did that mean these men came here together? "Did she say anything else?"

"That's the best part. Turn the paper over."

I did. On it was the list of three local companies. One was a road crew, another a painting contractor, and the third was our grocery store. "Is this where they work?"

"It is. She had to get references and work status in order to rent them their places."

Go, Christina. "This is awesome. You rock."

"Aw, thank you."

Once she left, Jaxson didn't look happy. "What's wrong? This is the break we've been looking for."

"Please tell me you aren't planning to go to their place of work and confront them? That might put a target on your back."

He could be such a party pooper sometimes. "I wouldn't do that." Or at least I wouldn't now that he mentioned how unsafe it could be. "You have to admit that the fact all three arrived in Witch's Cove at the same time is a bit suspicious."

"It is, which is why we should give the realtor a call to see where the men claimed to be from. If all three are from Montana, then Nash probably was the target—and still might be."

"That's logical."

Was it bad of me to be slightly relieved if that turned out to be the case, and there hadn't been some vindictive warlock after my cousin? Nash was not only a werewolf, he was a cop who could protect himself. Rihanna was merely a teenager. If she'd been able to make herself disappear at will, I might have felt better.

I snapped my fingers. "I have an idea."

"It better not be dangerous," Jaxson said.

"It might be, but only a little."

He blew out a breath and leaned back. "Tell me."

Iggy peeked his head out of my purse. "This should be good."

"While these men are at work, what if we check out the inside of their houses?"

"For the Spiderman costumes?" Iggy asked.

I stroked his head. "You are a true sleuth."

My iguana couldn't grin, but when he wiggled his upper body, it meant he was happy. "Thanks."

"Tell me, Glinda Goodall, when did you develop the skills to pick a lock?" my sassy partner asked.

"Have you forgotten about our talented friend, Levy?"

"Glinda, no," Jaxson said.

"Why not? He can cloak himself, unlock the door with his mind, and then sit in the car while we go in."

Jaxson craned his neck, acting as if I were crazy. "What if the owner returns? He's a freaking werewolf," he whispered. "We'd be shredded meat in seconds."

I held up a finger. "I thought of that. We'll ask Hunter to wait outside. He'll have our backs if anything happens."

"What is in your coffee? For starters, he'll never go for it. He was a cop at one time or close to it."

"He wants to stop this guy, too. Nash is his friend."

"Yes, but not by breaking and entering. Even if we found something, it couldn't be used in court."

"Spoilsport. What do you propose?" I asked.

"I'm good with doing a stakeout, but only to see if all three are still alive."

That was better than a hard no. "I'm good with that. If they all show up, it might prove they aren't our murdering werewolves."

"Not so fast, pink lady. They still could be. Who's to say that two of the three men didn't come across some unsuspecting hiker and kill him? The third friend could still be alive."

"You keep punching holes in my theories."

Jaxson grinned. "It's why we are partners."

He was my partner for other reasons, but I wasn't about to mention his strengths right now. "Regardless, it's worth checking it out. Besides, Rihanna has that telephoto lens on her camera."

"We aren't involving her," Jaxson shot back. "It could turn deadly."

They wouldn't recognize her. It was us they'd know. "Fine, but you and I have to go."

"I'm okay with that, as long as we don't break in. What are you going to tell Rihanna?"

I looked down at Iggy. "I don't know. Blabbermouth will tell her everything."

"I will not," Iggy said.

"Can she read your mind?" She could read mine, more or less.

"No."

That was good. "I still don't trust you." I wagged a finger at my familiar.

"Come on," Jaxson said. "Let's go back to the office and come up with a plan."

I'd just outlined a good one, but apparently it needed some refinement. Thankfully, we arrived before Rihanna returned home from school. He grabbed a water from the fridge and then motioned I take a seat on the sofa.

"I think we should call Christina to see what she can tell us about these men. She might know where they moved from," he said.

"Love it. Go for it." A woman would respond better to Jaxson anyway.

He called, but I could tell she must have had second thoughts about providing personal information about her clients, because Jaxson asked several times if they were from Montana. When he shook his head, I figured she wouldn't tell him.

He disconnected and huffed. "She isn't saying."

"That stinks."

"I know."

"Did we ever learn what these three men were wearing at the Halloween party after the murder? Steve or Misty took everyone's photo."

"Why does it matter?" he asked.

"It would be nice if someone remembers talking to them while they were dressed in these final costumes. Here's my theory: Suppose all three arrived wearing a Spiderman costume, and then when the lights went out, one of them murdered Peter. A second man helped lift the body into the casket while the third man threw the switch to cut the power. Then, in the chaos, they left."

"Wouldn't the Tiki Hut bartenders have seen them leave?" he asked.

"Without any lights?"

"The fire under the cauldron outside might have given off a glow."

I didn't even think of that. "Good point, but those two

bartenders looked pretty busy to me. They probably weren't watching who came and went."

"You might be right," he said.

"These three men could have changed into different costumes they'd stashed at the side of the building and then put their Spidermen costumes in the car," Iggy said, chiming in.

"I thought you said you didn't remember what they were wearing," I said.

"I didn't, but it's a theory."

I had to smile. We were tossing out theories right and left. He had every right to have his own. "You could be right, but I'm thinking it makes more sense that they'd change in their car—not in the open alleyway." Too bad we had no video cameras out there.

"I don't think so," Iggy said. "Maybe I was wrong in what I saw."

"Why don't you call your aunt and see if she can ask Pearl about these men and their costumes?"

I understood that if I asked Steve directly, he'd know I was going against his orders not to investigate. "Can do."

I called her and explained our request. "What reason should I give her for wanting to know about their outfits?" my aunt asked.

I had the phone on speaker, so I looked up at Jaxson hoping he'd have a suggestion.

"Tell her you remember talking to a few men when Peter was discussing something with Steve. You want to follow up with them," Jaxson said.

That was a good idea. I nodded.

"Okay. I'll call her and let you know."

"Thanks, Aunt Fern."

I disconnected. "Doesn't this case seem like all we do is wait for others to find the answers?"

"That's what sleuths do."

"No, it isn't. Sleuths do leg work to find the answers themselves." The office door opened, and Rihanna came in. "Hey," I said.

She stopped and studied us. "What happened?"

"Nothing, why?"

She shook her head and slung off her backpack. "Don't lie to me."

I looked over at Jaxson, hoping once more he'd know what to say.

"Why don't you change and then come out here. We have something to tell you," he said.

"That's better."

Rihanna was quick to freshen up. On her way out, she grabbed a drink and then joined us. "What happened? And please don't sugarcoat it. I'll know if you do."

"Fine. Someone was mauled to death by two werewolves today," I announced.

Her face paled. "Who was it?"

We explained that we didn't know. "Hunter thinks the victim was a werewolf."

"Was he one of the men at the party?" she asked.

"Again, we don't know." I told her about Steve asking the gossip queens to narrow down the party list. They were familiar with all but three people. The good news is that we've learned where they live."

Jaxson chugged his drink. "It's why we want to stake out the three men, in part to see if all three are alive. If one doesn't show up, he might be the murdered man."

Or there could be another plausible explanation. Ugh. I hated all of this uncertainty. It made me reconsider my career choice.

Rihanna's eyes shone. "I can help."

"No," he said.

"Why not? I promise not to get out of my car. I've done other stakeouts for you. I know enough to leave if I see trouble."

Jaxson hesitated. He turned to me. "What do you think?"

He was the one who didn't want Rihanna to go in the first place. I wonder what had changed his mind, but I'm glad he was considering it. "We could use the help, and she hasn't been caught yet while on stakeout." Rihanna had helped twice in the past.

"Okay, but I want us to be in constant communication, and you must keep your car doors locked at all times, Rihanna."

My cousin grinned. "Of course."

"Please realize that if they see you, they might kill you." I wanted to scare her.

"Don't worry. I'll use my 300mm lens and stay far away. If I balance it on the car window, I'll get great pictures."

"Sounds good."

"Just to be sure, what is our goal? Merely to take their picture?" she asked.

Good question. "We partly want to see if all three men show up at home tonight. If one of them doesn't, we might conclude two of them killed the third man." I held up a palm. "I know it's a stretch. There could be other werewolves wandering the forest, but it wasn't a full moon last night."

"I believe these men were responsible for killing Peter Upton," Jaxson added. "No proof. Just gut."

"Good enough for me. When do we leave?" Rihanna asked, more excited than I'd seen her in a while.

## Chapter Ten

WE HAD RIHANNA follow us to the first house we'd checked out. It belonged to Travis Knowlton. There were fewer homes in this neighborhood, but it was the best area of the three.

During our drive, I stayed in contact with Rihanna. She had her cell on speaker so we both could communicate with her. Once she parked, we pulled up next to her, and I rolled down the window. "That's the house."

"Yes, you showed me the video."

So I had. "If you see anything suspicious, leave." I know I sounded like her mother, but she was my responsibility.

"I'll be okay." She patted her fancy camera that was cradled in her lap.

"Call us anytime."

She smiled. "I'll be fine. Go."

Jaxson chuckled as he pulled away. The next apartment complex was about a mile away. It only had four units, and George Fredericks had rented Unit A. There were two cars in the lot, but we didn't know if one belonged to him or not. If only Steve had been more forthcoming with his information, we would know more.

If the man showed up—which I suspected he would—

Jaxson planned to duck down to avoid suspicion, while I would pretend to be waiting for someone.

"Should we check in with Rihanna?" I asked less than a half hour later.

Jaxson glanced over at me. "She is an adult who can handle herself."

He didn't have that opinion when we were at the coffeeshop, but I didn't comment on it. "She's only eighteen. I should have gone with her."

The rumble of an engine neared, and Jaxson glanced up at the rear view mirror. "Heads up," he said.

I lifted my phone, ready to take his picture. He might be George Fredericks, and he might not be. When the new arrival got out of his blue truck that he'd parked close to the apartment, I snapped a picture of the back of his bald head. So much for being able to photograph his face, but his lack of hair might help identify him. He walked up to Unit A, opened the door, and went in. My breath caught. "It's him."

"I'll make a note of his license plate number." Jaxson was always cool under pressure.

"Good."

Then we waited. For what, I wasn't sure. When he didn't come out in the next five minutes, I had to ask Jaxson why we were still here. "Are you expecting him to do something?"

"No. I wanted to give him a minute to settle in. It would look obvious if we left right away."

"Got it." I had a lot to learn about stakeouts.

After another minute or two, we left to check out the second man, Tony DeLorenzo. He had a job at the grocery store, so there was no way to know what hours he worked.

Considering he lived in a two-story apartment building, we might learn nothing. I suspected a lot of people would be coming and going in this large complex. Not only that, we didn't know what he looked like, which put us at a disadvantage. At some point, I might have to beg Steve to look at the photos of these three men.

Knowing how long these stakeouts could last, I'd brought a cooler with some drinks and snacks. I pulled out a water. "Want one?"

"Thanks."

We'd been there maybe ten minutes, when my cell rang. When I saw it was Rihanna, my heart immediately plummeted. I answered quickly. "Are you okay?"

"Yes, but some guy in a blue Toyota truck with a red stripe down the side just pulled up to Travis' house. He just went into the house with some other guy. The good news is that I recognized the one who wasn't the driver. I remember him from the party because of his red hair."

That was good information. She was on speaker, so I looked over at Jaxson. He didn't say a word. Instead, Jaxson started the car. "We'll be right there," I announced before disconnecting. "If George is at Travis' house with a partygoer, those three must be friends."

Jaxson nodded. "The question we need to ask ourselves is whether their connection has anything to do with Peter's death. They could have heard about the Halloween party and gone together."

"It's always possible." I hoped not though. "Otherwise it might mean Rihanna and Levy were back in the spotlight. It would also mean that whoever killed Peter, would have to be someone the Witch's Cove community knew and trusted."

"That would be a real shame," he said.

After a short drive, Jaxson pulled up next to Rihanna. Yes, he'd stopped in the middle of the road, but there weren't any cars, so we'd be fine for the moment—assuming no one was watching us. I rolled down the window. "Anything new?" I asked her.

"No."

Jaxson leaned across me. "We'll pull in front of you and park."

"I can handle it," Rihanna said.

"I know, but Glinda is too nosy to leave," he said without asking me. That was okay. It was the truth.

She smiled. "Got it."

Once Jaxson shut off the engine, we settled back to wait. The house lights were on, and I'd occasionally see someone move inside. Was Travis having an afterwork party? Or were they plotting something together? I know, I know. It wasn't fair to assume these guys had harmed anyone without proof, but gut instincts didn't lie.

"Maybe we should head out," I said. "I imagine Rihanna got some good shots of the two men going into his house, which is probably good enough to prove the three of them are friends. Steve will be able to tell us if the man with George is Tony DeLorenzo."

"I agree. We just don't have any proof they are guilty of anything. Call and tell her we need to head out," he said.

I dialed Rihanna and told her we were leaving. These men might be there all night, and she had school tomorrow.

"I thought you believed these guys had something to do

with Mr. Upton's death."

"We did think that, but since they all seem to be alive, I don't think these are our murdering werewolves."

"Something's been bugging me," Rihanna said.

"What's that?"

"Where is Mr. Knowlton's car?" she asked.

I had assumed it was in the garage, but when I looked, the house didn't have one. "Good question."

Before I could ask Jaxson, the front door opened, and two men came out carrying two suitcases each. What the heck?

"Take their picture quick," Jaxson said. He ducked down so I could get a clear shot, even though Rihanna would be doing a better job.

The men tossed the suitcases in the back of the blue truck and then returned inside. "What do you think they are doing?" I asked.

"I'm not about to ask them."

"This is a bit out there, but maybe they killed Travis and now want the landlord to think the guy moved."

He nodded. "That seems reasonable."

My cell rang. "Yes, Rihanna?"

"What are they doing?"

"I'd like to know myself. Why don't you head back? I don't want them to get suspicious that there are two cars parked in front of the house."

"Okay." She disconnected.

I hadn't expected her to react like that. Fearless Rihanna must be scared. She pulled next to us, looked over, and then continued. For a change, I didn't say anything, but I had a feeling this Travis guy might be dead.

Fifteen minutes later, the men carried out a couple of trash bags, full of what I didn't know. "Maybe we should call Hunter."

"Who will call Nash. Are you okay with Steve knowing that we interfered?"

"It won't be anything new. I think we are a bit over our heads on this." I never liked admitting something like that, but in this case, it was true. These men might be werewolves after all.

"This could be innocent, you know."

"I don't get the sense these men are the type to pack up a friend's belongings."

Jaxson stilled, his gaze nowhere in particular. "Travis could be inside, directing them."

"Maybe. I'm calling Hunter. If these guys leave town, we may never catch them."

"What if Travis is already in Montana waiting for his friends?"

"He would have packed his own things."

"Maybe he had an emergency, and his friends volunteered to pack for him," Jaxson said.

Ugh. "I could call his employer and ask if Travis showed up to work today. I could say I was his girlfriend and was worried about him. The boss would know if there had been an emergency in his employee's life."

Jaxson checked his phone. "Travis worked for a painting company. They'll be closed right now."

I didn't want these guys to get away with something—assuming they were guilty. "Then I'll call Hunter and ask him what he thinks."

"Fine, but be fast. These guys may not be here for long."

I made the call. "Hunter, it's Glinda. Hear me out before you say anything." I detailed the series of events leading up to us watching what I guessed was the final clearing out of Travis Knowlton's house. "It is probably a stretch, but what if George and Tony killed Travis and are packing up to make it look like he left town?"

"Give me the address." Hunter sounded highly focused and didn't ask me any questions or tell me I shouldn't be there.

I gave him the information. "Should we follow them to see what they are going to do with the stuff?"

"No. You guys go home. I'll ask Nash to help. What kind of car are they driving?"

I gave them the details and the license plate number. "Let me know what happens."

"Will do. And Glinda?"

"Yes?"

"Thank you and stay safe."

"We will." I then nodded to Jaxson. "Time to go."

"The men are leaving. I hope Hunter and Nash can find them."

The timing was bad, but it couldn't be helped. "If they think they are being followed, they won't go where they'd planned anyway."

"Which was where?" he asked.

"I have no idea, but if I'd killed my friend, I'd try to get rid of his things. Having his possessions would incriminate me."

"True. Text Hunter and tell him they are headed north

toward Seminole Boulevard."

"Will do."

There were a lot of blue trucks on the road, but not many with a red stripe down the side. After the two men were out of sight, we took off. I wanted to look in the windows, but Jaxson thought it better that we not.

---

"IT'S BEEN THREE hours," I whined.

"Hunter said he'd call when he learned anything."

"If he and Nash never located them, he would have called already, so the lack of contact might be a good thing."

"Which means they did find them and are now on stakeout," Jaxson said.

Rihanna walked in from her room. "Maybe we should call Steve and ask him."

"I'm sure Nash mentioned his little side trip to our sheriff, but on the off chance he didn't, I want to wait," I said.

Rihanna shrugged. "Okay."

"Do you want to do a little slideshow for us of your photos?" I was sure her pictures were much better than mine.

"Sure. I'll get my computer."

She returned a minute later, connected a cord to her camera, and pressed play. Rihanna had a few videos. One was of the two men arriving and then of them entering the house.

"Is it me, or didn't they even knock?" I asked.

"They didn't knock," Jaxson confirmed. "They clearly knew their friend wasn't home."

"Play it again," I told Rihanna. "How are they getting

into the house? I shudder to think they are as talented as our other warlocks who could open doors with their minds."

Jaxson leaned closer and then stopped the video. "There. He has a kit in his hand. It's what he used to pick the lock."

"Interesting."

We watched the rest of the video, but I didn't remember seeing them at the party. They must have had their faces covered for most of the time. When Steve, Nash, and Misty were interviewing everyone, I was guarding the door. Besides, the large crowd made it difficult to see much anyway.

My cell rang, causing my heart to almost stop when I saw the caller ID. "Hunter?"

"Glinda. It's bad."

My hands shook as I put my cell on speaker. "What happened?"

"Nash and I followed the men to the woods and then lost them."

That was disappointing for sure but not terrible. "They have to come out of the woods eventually."

"Oh, they did."

He wasn't making any sense.

"Were they there to ditch all of Travis' belongings?" Jaxson asked.

"Maybe that had been their plan, but when they saw us, they attacked. Nash is seriously injured."

Oh, no.

## Chapter Eleven

"How bad is Nash?" I asked.

"Bad. I have gouges on my back and legs, but they are nothing like his injuries."

I never should have called Hunter. I had a suspicion these men were dangerous. "I am so sorry. This is all my fault."

"No, it's not."

"I should have come home and let the men go their merry way. It was the idea of them returning to wherever they came from without any punishment that made me want them stopped."

"You did the right thing in calling me. I'm thankful you and Jaxson didn't follow them yourselves."

He didn't need to state why. We might have ended up dead.

"What happened to the men as a result of the battle?" Jaxson asked.

"They sustained some injuries, but they are not nearly as bad as the two of us."

I thought both Hunter and Nash were great fighters. "How did they beat you?"

I know that was a tacky thing to ask, but I had a suspicion about something and wanted it confirmed.

"We were taken by surprise. Neither of us smelled a thing. The worst part was that they attacked us while we were in our human form. By the time we managed to shift—which was no easy feat—we'd lost a lot of our strength."

The three of us looked at each other, horror written on both Rihanna's and Jaxson's faces. "They have to be stopped," I proclaimed, though I knew I wouldn't be the one to do it.

"We plan to try," Hunter said.

By *we*, I was guessing that meant Heather since Nash wouldn't be fighting anytime soon. I could only hope that his assistant was a fierce fighter. "Where are you guys now?"

"With Dr. Sanchez."

She was our medical examiner. "Why not go to the hospital?"

"Glinda, Witch's Cove isn't ready for another animal attack. I already worry there will come a day when wolves are killed on sight—as in all wolves, including werewolves."

I, more than anyone, understood how horrible that would be. I was extremely thankful that my father was immune from shifting, but many others were not. "What can we do?"

"Nothing for now. Steve is here with Nash. Don't worry, he'll figure something out."

But Steve lacked certain abilities that might help—like that of being a werewolf. "Did you see their faces at all?"

"No. They were in their wolf form the whole time."

"Are they still in the woods, do you think?" Jaxson asked.

"I have no idea. If I were them, I doubt that I would return to my house. We did scratch both of them pretty good. Those marks will be visible for a few days until their wolf has had time to heal them."

"Have you told Penny what happened?" I asked.

"No. I'd rather she not see me for a few days until my wounds heal. You know her. She'd fall to pieces."

Sad to say, that was true. I know if anything happened to Jaxson or Rihanna, I'd be the same way. "I'll say nothing—for now."

"Thank you. Look, I gotta go."

"Okay. Thanks for letting us know."

When he disconnected, my body was numb. "I can't believe they were ambushed," I said.

Jaxson scooted next to me on the sofa and wrapped an arm around my shoulders. "It seems that way. This could have been those werewolves' plan all along."

"Their plan? How? They had no idea we'd find out where they lived or that we'd do some kind of stakeout and then have them followed."

He shrugged. "Maybe. It's possible they made sure that Heather or Hunter saw them going into the woods and hoped they'd call Nash."

"That makes more sense to me," Rihanna said.

It did to me, too. "I wish we had some kind of infrared drone that could see their heat signature in the forest so we could find them."

"If we called in the military, I bet they'd have a drone to do what you want, but telling them we're looking for two werewolves might cause them to lock us up in a psych ward," Jaxson said.

"You're no help. Then what?"

Rihanna's cell rang. She picked it up and smiled. "It's Gavin. Excuse me."

Gavin, huh? "Maybe he knows something."

"Glinda," Jaxson said with a chastising tone.

"What? It wouldn't hurt to ask him."

Rihanna headed to her room. "I'll try." She swiped the phone. "Hey, Gavin."

As soon as she closed her door, we couldn't hear anything. Darn. Chances were, he was with his mom in the morgue helping to take care of Nash and probably Hunter. I hoped the good doctor had supplies to help them. Considering all of her patients were dead, she might not have a stocked first aid kit. Or would she? She was a medical doctor.

The one plus was that Steve and Nash had told her about werewolves a few months back.

Iggy crawled between us. "Maybe I can find these werewolves," he said. "Like I did the last time."

Jaxson picked him up and placed him on his lap. "We appreciate it, bud, but the forest is thousands of acres. They might even be on the move."

"They could be on their way back to Montana for all we know," I tossed in.

"Nope," Iggy said. "Nash is still alive. They aren't going anywhere until he's dead."

How did he know? "That's a terrible thought, but injuring Nash enough to teach him a lesson might be good enough for them."

He closed his eyes, as if to say end of discussion.

"We've got to figure out a way to help Heather and Hunter find these guys," I said.

"To do that, we'd need a spell," Jaxson suggested.

"Yes, a spell that even Gertrude doesn't know if it exists or not."

He waved a dismissive hand. "Bad idea. We should abandon that line of thinking."

I knew what was coming. "Why? Because it's too dangerous? That the only way to do the spell is to be close to these guys, and if they sense me, they might take me out?"

"Smart girl. Not only that, what if the spell is successful?"

What if? Okay, to be fair, not all of my spells have worked. "Then Hunter and Nash, when he recovers, can follow them."

"And these men will be able to follow them back."

I didn't like that. "They probably can do that now. How else did George and Tony even know that Nash and Hunter were in the forest?"

"I'd be guessing, but they might have expected a tail. Who's to say whether Hunter is any good at following discretely, or not?"

"You might be right."

Rihanna's bedroom door opened, and she came out. I tried to judge her mood, but I couldn't. "What did Gavin say?"

She sat down. "He was amazingly forthcoming."

"That's great."

"For starters, the man who was mauled was Travis Knowlton."

That proved one thing: one of the three men from the party was dead. There was no proof his two cohorts were the werewolves who killed him though. "That's good to know, but is Dr. Sanchez sure?"

"Yes. If I understand the process correctly, she compared

Travis's driver's license photo, along with the photo the sheriff took, to a photo of his face. It was really cool. She knows Photoshop."

"How did that help, considering his face was torn up?"

"The short of it was she took a picture of his rather messed up face, and then superimposed it over each of the other good photos. The eyes, nose, and mouth lined up."

"That's great." I looked over at Jaxson. "Did he happen to mention if the facial injuries happened after death."

She held up a finger. "Yes, he did, and yes they were."

"That is good to know. It implies someone really didn't want Travis' identity known. Unless more werewolves are living in the forest, his two friends might have killed him."

"Let's not jump to conclusions," Jaxson said. "It wasn't that long ago that the clan who murdered Diamond Dirk were in the forest. Who's to say they aren't still there and are responsible? They might not like interlopers."

"You could be right. For the moment, I'm more interested in figuring out who killed Peter, and whether George and Tony are the men who attacked our two friends than learning if they killed Travis."

"I agree."

I turned back to Rihanna. "Did Gavin tell you how Hunter and Nash are doing? From the way Hunter sounded, he too, was injured pretty badly."

She nodded. "Hunter will live, but Dr. Sanchez says it's touch and go for Nash. He's not healing like he should."

My heart nearly burst. "I thought werewolves had super healing power."

"I wouldn't know," Rihanna said.

"I'd ask my dad, but he might not know either." Other than Nash, Hunter, and Heather, I didn't know any other werewolves to ask. Even if Hunter's new assistant said werewolves healed faster, what difference would it make?

"Is there some kind of spell that would help him heal faster?" Jaxson asked.

"A healing spell?" I asked. "I've never heard of one."

"What if these men are part warlock and put a curse on Nash and Hunter that prevent them from healing?" Rihanna asked.

That thought churned my stomach. "What can we do if they did?"

"Rihanna is onto something. What was done might be able to be undone. Get it? Levy or Gertrude might be able to help."

"There's a better chance of finding something like that than me healing someone."

Jaxson stood and faced my cousin. "I think we've had enough excitement for one day. I'll walk Glinda home, and then I'm going to spend the night here again."

"You don't have to do that," Rihanna said. "Those men clearly aren't after me or Levy. We've more or less proven they are werewolves."

Jaxson pointed a finger at her. "It's the more or less part that worries me. Besides, I like being near both of you. Don't forget, they could be part warlock."

I wasn't going to argue with him. I, too, liked when Jaxson was near. "Works for me."

I gathered Iggy and then said goodnight to Rihanna. Once we left, I was still worried about Nash, but knowing that my cousin would be safe calmed me a bit.

"Do you really think there is a spell that can cancel a curse that prevents healing?" I asked Jaxson.

"I'm not the one to ask."

"Tomorrow, if Nash isn't improving, I will certainly give Levy a call." As usual, Jaxson escorted me upstairs to my apartment. "Do you want to come in for a drink?"

He smiled and then ran a thumb down my cheek. "Another time, pink lady. I don't want Rihanna to worry if I don't return right away."

I could understand that. "Thank you." I hugged him goodnight.

"Sleep well." He kissed the top of my head and then stepped back.

As soon as he went downstairs, I headed inside.

"Is Nash going to be okay?" Iggy asked, sounding rather worried.

"I certainly hope so."

"Are you going to ask Gertrude or Levy about a spell to help Nash?"

I couldn't remember when my familiar had been this upset. My mind was too stressed out right now to wonder why. "As soon as I see for myself how he is doing, I'll decide." I thought I'd already mentioned that to Jaxson. Iggy must not have been paying attention. "I'm heading to bed."

"I want to talk to Aimee," he said.

I liked that he thought his cat girlfriend could help his anxiety, but I didn't want the two of them disturbing Aunt Fern. "You can invite her over here if you're going to chat."

"Okay."

No surprise, I didn't sleep much, and I really needed to be clear headed today. The best thing I could do was eat a good breakfast, something I rarely took the time to do in the morning. Since it was quite early, I thought Dr. Sanchez's office might not even be open—unless she'd received another body.

Iggy said he'd head on over to the office when he felt like it. "Don't forget, Jaxson might be downstairs working, and Rihanna is at school."

"I know, but most of the action happens there," he said.

He was right about that. I went downstairs and grabbed a table in Penny's section. Aunt Fern was chatting with someone at the check-out counter. If I didn't know better, it was almost as if nothing had happened, except that the decorations were still there—like the mannequins, the pumpkins, and the cemetery. The pumpkins might last a bit longer, but eventually they would rot. I needed to see about putting everything away—just not right now.

Penny rushed over. "Hey. Hunter called and said Nash was in a fight?"

I stilled. Did he fail to say he'd been there, too? I would have given her the details, but I didn't want to rat him out. "Yes. I'm going to check on Nash right after this."

"Tell him I send my best."

"I will."

Before she could ask any more questions I didn't want to answer, I ordered some pancakes with a side of fruit. "And coffee, of course."

She smiled. "I'll bring plenty of cream and sugar."

Penny knew me well. Right after my friend delivered my breakfast, Aunt Fern came over. "Pearl got back to me."

I wasn't sure what the last thing was I'd asked her. "Great. What did she say?"

"The three men, Travis Knowlton, George Fredericks, and Tony DeLorenzo were wearing Batman, Olaf, and Darth Vader costumes when Steve took their picture."

"Tell her thank you. I remember checking in an Olaf, but not the other two, though we saw a lot of people."

She stepped closer. "You heard about Nash and Hunter, right?" I was thankful she kept her voice down for a change.

"Yes. I'm heading over to Dr. Sanchez's office as soon as I finish eating."

"I heard it's bad."

My appetite disappeared. "That was this morning?"

"Yes. Nash's *animal* isn't healing him."

Hunter must have explained that it would by now. "Rihanna suggested that someone might have put a curse on Nash that prevented him from healing."

She sucked in a breath. "That's terrible."

"I know. I want to see if Gertrude or Levy can help."

My aunt squeezed my shoulder. "I'm so glad they have you looking out for them."

I hoped that would be a benefit instead of another curse.

## Chapter Twelve

I GENTLY KNOCKED on Dr. Sanchez's door before entering her office, but she wasn't there. If Nash, and possibly Hunter were somewhere close by, where would that be? I'd never explored the morgue to know if there were other rooms.

I stepped into the hallway. "Hello?"

No answer. Where were they? Had Nash flatlined or something, and Dr. Sanchez had to take him to the Emergency Room? I shivered at that thought. I had the doctor's number. While I didn't want to disturb her, I wanted to learn how Nash was doing. After some indecision, I called her.

"Glinda?" she answered.

"Yes. How are Nash and Hunter?"

"Hunter should be okay, but Nash is unconscious."

My soul nearly squeezed out of me. "I need to see him."

She hesitated. "That's not a good idea."

I had to make her understand. "I have no proof, but it's possible the werewolves who attacked Nash and Hunter put a curse on them—or at least on Nash." I honestly didn't know if a curse could be directed at only one person if someone else was close by—someone like Hunter.

"A curse to do what?" she asked with disbelief in her voice.

"To prevent them from healing."

"Glinda. As a woman of science, I find curses very hard to believe."

"I get it, but as a woman of science, I bet you never thought werewolves existed either, right?"

Her breathing increased, but she said nothing for a moment. "You're right."

"I'm sure Hunter told you that werewolves have an amazing ability to heal themselves."

"He told me that," she said. "So far, I haven't seen any evidence of it."

"That's because if there is a curse on these men, they won't be able to heal."

"Then you might be right about there being a curse."

"Do you think I could talk to Hunter for just a minute? I want to find a way to cancel this spell, though there are no guarantees something like a reversal even exists. I need some information."

"Fine, but you can't stay long."

A bit of hope trickled in. "Of course. Where are they?"

"They are at my house." She gave me her address, and I entered it into my phone.

"I'm on my way."

I texted Jaxson to let him know my status. If there had been a lot of time, I might have spoken to Gertrude first, but I wanted to ask Hunter some questions before I wasted anyone's time.

Once outside, I hopped in my car and headed over to Dr. Sanchez's house, which was only about ten minutes from her office. Even before I slipped out of my car, she had opened the front door. I rushed up the driveway to greet her.

Dr. Sanchez held up a hand. "I need to warn you that Nash's leg is badly injured and is not pleasant to look at. You need to be prepared not to show horror—for Hunter's sake."

An unconscious Nash wouldn't know, but for Hunter's sake, I would try. "I've seen my share of mangled dead bodies, but when it's someone who's alive, I can only promise to do my best."

She nodded. I followed the doctor past the living room and kitchen to a hallway. She lightly tapped on a closed door and then pushed it open. Hunter was in one bed, half his body propped up, while Nash was pale, and his arms and legs were heavily bandaged. It was clear from the color of his face and the severity of the other exposed wounds that this man was on borrowed time. My heart nearly broke.

While the doctor went over to check on Nash, I sat in the chair next to Hunter's bed. "How are you feeling?"

Yes, it was a dumb question. If he'd been good, he wouldn't have been here.

"I'll heal."

"Are you sure? I mean are you healing at the same rate as usual?"

He glanced away. "No, and that is a problem."

"I think I know why." His brow rose. "One of the men might have put a curse on you and Nash."

"A curse." His statement made it sound as if he didn't believe in them either, but he had to know something was wrong.

"Yes. We talked about these werewolves possibly being able to cloak their scent, remember?"

"Sure, but most likely they had a witch put a spell on them to block it."

We had drawn that conclusion. "Now, I'm thinking these men might be part warlock, which makes them much more dangerous."

"In what way?"

"It's possible they put a curse on you and Nash that prevents you from healing. It might be blocking your animal abilities. I don't know exactly."

He sucked in a breath. "Someone can do that?"

"Maybe. I'm not all that well-versed in warlock stuff. I'm thinking this curse might even be designed to make all wounds worse."

Hunter huffed. "Aren't you the cheery one."

"Sorry." I looked over at Nash whose breathing was shallow. "I doubt they had time to perform a spell before they attacked, though it is possible. Can you tell me what happened?"

"There's not much more than what I told you over the phone. We were searching for them when they just appeared in their wolf form. The wolves growled and then attacked. Unless they did a spell when they were out of sight, I don't think they had time once they were near. Even if I believe humans can perform magic, I don't imagine werewolves can."

"Without hands, it might be hard, but if they are part warlock, I don't know what they are capable of."

"How long would this spell take to cast? Or better yet, how long would it last? They could have said it before they shifted or put it on us a while ago, knowing that if we were ever injured, we wouldn't heal."

I was afraid he'd ask me this. "I have to be honest, I haven't investigated it enough. I will talk to Gertrude and Levy Poole when I'm done here, but if it is like most spells, it would take longer than a few seconds to invoke. As for how long it can last, the spell I put on Jaxson to enable him to communicate with Iggy is still working, but the spell to have super hearing and sight has worn off. It appears to be a hit or miss."

He ran a hand through his hair. "So now what?"

"I'm hoping there is something I can do to reverse this curse."

He nodded over to Nash. "You better hurry. I don't know how long he can hang on."

"I am worried about that, too. By chance, did either of you two spend any time talking to either a Spiderman, Olaf, Batman, or Darth Vader at the party?"

"You're joking, right?"

"Why would I joke?"

"Sorry, it's just that we talked to a lot of people, and Penny and I checked in about twenty partygoers."

"I was thinking more like when you went inside. It appears as if these men planned their attack carefully, from cloaking their scent to putting a curse on Nash should he survive their assault. Their only error—or so I believe—was in killing the wrong man."

"Dr. Sanchez said that the murdered man Heather found was Travis Knowlton, a friend of the other two."

"I know. If his two partners killed him, we may never learn why. My guess would be that they don't tolerate mistakes."

"Nice friends."

I appreciated that Hunter could kind of joke at a time like this. "I know I said I only had one more question, but was there any time when you and Nash were together at the party? That's when they might have put the curse on Nash, and it extended to you. I imagine one of them distracted you two while another said the spell."

His eyes lit up, and he then shook a finger. "Yes. Penny was talking to you for a bit, so I chatted with Nash."

"Spells don't have pinpoint accuracy, at least the ones I know about don't. These men could have done some incantation toward all werewolves in the room."

"Including your father?"

My stomach churned. "Yes, including my father."

Hunter shook his head. "They didn't know we were ones either. If they did, they wouldn't have mistakenly killed Peter."

"I think they knew at least who Nash was, but they somehow got their wires crossed during the execution of their plan. The lights were flashing those ghosts on the ceiling, so it wasn't easy to see in there. Maybe they identified Nash as someone who was wearing a vampire costume, but when the crowd grew, they got him mixed up."

"My head is spinning from this. Let's assume you are right in that these men wanted to be positive that Nash would die even after being stabbed. Where do we go from here?"

"Like I said, I'm going to ask Gertrude or Levy about this cancellation spell," I said.

"Are you hopeful it will work?"

"I won't know until I try it. Curses are often two-way

streets, so to speak. If a witch or warlock can cast a spell, it can be broken. I just have to find someone who knows how to do this."

"Which is why you want to talk to Levy. He is a warlock," Hunter said.

"Yes. If—or rather when Nash wakes up—tell him to hold on. I'm doing my best."

Hunter leaned over and hugged me. "Thank you."

I smiled—or as close to a smile as I could muster. "If anything happened to you, Penny would be a basket case. For my own sanity, you know I have to do everything I can to make you better."

Hunter tapped his fingers to his forehead. "To Penny."

On the way out, I told Dr. Sanchez that I would do what I could to help both men. "They just need to hang on a little longer."

"Thank you, Glinda."

When I left, I had this sinking feeling that I had promised more than I could deliver. While Gertrude might be able to help, considering she hadn't called about the uncloaking spell yet, I thought I would speak with Levy first.

Once in my car, I called him and explained that Hunter and Nash had been attacked by two werewolves. "The problem is that my two friends haven't healed. In fact, Nash may not survive."

"I am so sorry."

"Thank you. I'm thinking one of the werewolves put a curse on both men that prevents them from healing. Have you heard of anything like that?"

"No."

I was pinning much of my hope on Levy. If he couldn't help, I don't know what I would do. "Is there anyone you can ask?"

I could almost hear his mind whirring. "I can gather our coven leaders if you want to address them. Coming from you, it might have more impact."

Me? My mother was a member of a coven, but I never felt I was good enough to belong. According to Levy's grandmother, his coven was much more powerful than the one my mom belonged to in Witch's Cove. His group could read people's minds—more or less—and open locks mentally. And that was probably a small portion of their talent, but if I said no, Nash would die.

"Where and when should I meet you?" He gave me the time and place. "I'll be there."

Since I had about twenty minutes to spare, I called Jaxson.

"How are they?" he asked.

I explained that it didn't look good for Nash. "Levy has set up a meeting with his coven right now. It's possible one of them might know how to reverse the curse."

"Is there anything I can do?"

I loved how supportive he was. "I can't think of anything."

"Then good luck."

I would need more than luck. I disconnected and headed for a drive-thru restaurant since I needed a strong cup of coffee if I was going to make it through a coven meeting. I'd been to a few meetings with my mom, but that was when I was in high school. I honestly didn't know what to expect from this one.

Thankfully, the meeting place was easy to find, though I didn't expect them to be meeting in what looked like a library. Levy was standing out front waiting for me. I parked and walked up to him. "Hey."

He seemed to analyze me. It took a moment to realize he was trying to get a reading off of what I was thinking. If he'd asked, I could have told him: I was petrified and afraid of Nash dying because I'd messed up. If I hadn't called Hunter in the first place, none of this would have happened.

"The entrance is on the side. Most of the leaders have arrived." He looked over me and smiled. "Don't worry. They don't bite."

That made me smile. "You can tell I'm nervous?"

"What do you think?"

That would be an affirmative. I expected there to be a door handle, but there wasn't. Levy placed a palm on a sensor and leaned forward. "This place has an eye scanner?"

"When you go inside, you'll see why we have the need for such security."

"I get security, but why not have a lock that only the mind can open?"

"Ah, I understand. You think that because a few of us can open locks that way, everyone can. Most can't. Turns out we each have our own distinctive talents. It's what makes our coven so powerful."

"Good to know." *Here goes nothing.*

## Chapter Thirteen

THE ROOM LEVY led me to wasn't very large, but it was filled with tall bookcases that contained ancient looking tomes. Sconces, fueled by what I guessed contained propane, lit the room in a yellow glow. It wouldn't have surprised me if the members had been dressed in ancient robes or something, but they weren't. In fact, the six-person assembly looked rather ordinary. Two men were in business suits, while two more were dressed in jeans and T-shirts. The women wore slacks and nice blouses. Considering it was mid-day, it looked as if this might be their lunch hour.

Levy introduced me. "Time is of utmost importance. The deputy in Witch's Cove, a werewolf, is clinging to life after having been attacked by some werewolves." He explained about the possible reason for the attack. "Both he and his former partner, now a forest ranger, were injured. Neither are healing from their wounds." Levy looked over at me, as if it was now my turn to ask for their help.

"Hi, as Levy said, I'm Glinda." As a former school teacher, speaking in front of a group never bothered me, but for some reason being in front of this group did. Their power scared me. I couldn't help but think they could read my mind. I inhaled, forcing my thoughts to settle. "I believe two werewolves put an anti-healing curse on these two men. I'm really hoping someone has an idea how I can break the spell."

All of them looked around. "Camila, any thoughts?" Levy asked. He turned to me. "Camila is a werewolf and a witch."

This must have been the reason he believed his coven could help.

"I've never heard of this particular curse, but it is possible there is one. As for reversing it, I imagine that exists, too." She pushed back from the table and walked over to the bookshelves.

There were hundreds of books that I could have spent years looking through. Even if I read each one, I wouldn't remember where I found which spell—assuming that's what these books were.

She grabbed one and leafed through it. "Here it is. I thought I'd seen it before. Unfortunately, there is no mention of an antidote."

I tried not to let my disappointment show. "How difficult was this spell to cast?" I wanted to see if one or two of the werewolves could have done the incantation in the middle of a party without anyone noticing.

"It's easy, if you possess the right powers." She looked over at Levy. "Opening locks with his mind is easy for Levy but impossible for me. As I'm sure you are aware, doing a spell is much easier than undoing it, which is as it should be. Otherwise, it would mean anyone could negate our powers."

"That makes sense."

One of the men in a suit pushed back his chair. "Time is of the essence. Let's all look."

The entire group participated, pouring over the books. I

might have taken part had I'd known what to look for. Less than fifteen minutes later, a man in blue jeans placed a book on the table. "Look at this."

They huddled around and silently read it. Camila smiled. "That's it. Glinda, have a seat." She looked up at Levy. "Can you get something we can take notes on?"

Levy went over to a desk and retrieved a piece of paper and pencil. From the length of the spell, this looked complicated. I hoped I had the ability to perform this.

"You'll need quite a few ingredients." Camila listed what was needed. "Most of these will be found in the woods, but you'll need help locating them, unless you are an expert in botany."

"Hardly. May I see?"

She slipped me the paper. I recognized pine needles and an oak leaf, but where in the world might I find a sassafras root? "Do you think all of these exist around here?"

She shrugged. "I've never looked."

My hope was that Hex and Bones could provide me with some of the items. "This spell is in what language?"

Reciting in English was hard enough, let alone in something I couldn't understand.

She glanced down at the ancient book. "I can't be sure, but considering the age of this book, maybe some dead Latin language mixed with Celtic. I imagine most of the words don't even exist today."

Great. "Please don't tell me if I mispronounce one word, all will be lost."

"Hopefully not. Your innate abilities are what's most important."

The urge to laugh was strong. My innate abilities? "Do you think you could do it for me?"

She shook her head. "I would in a heartbeat if I thought it would work, but it says in the book that the spell giver must have a personal connection to the person or persons who were cursed."

That was what Bertha said when I asked about a locator spell. "Okay, I'll try. I can't thank you all enough for taking time out of your busy day to help me."

"Our pleasure. Please let Levy know how it goes," Camila said.

"I will."

With my spell and list of ingredients in hand, Levy escorted me out. Once more he had to place his palm on some sensor plate and use an eye scanner to get out. Because of the powerful books in this room, I could understand the caution.

After I thanked him, I headed back to town, though I wasn't quite sure where to stop first. I suppose Bertha's store would be my best bet since some of the items on the list seemed ancient. I would tell her mostly the truth—just not about Nash and Hunter being werewolves.

I parked in front of Hex and Bones Apothecary and entered. I still had nightmares from the time I stopped in and learned Bertha was off visiting her ill sister. Her substitute was the one who gave me the wrong ingredients for my requested spell. Instead of turning Iggy back to green, we both ended up with the ability to see ghosts. In retrospect, it turned out to be a good thing.

Inside the store, Bertha was there, and I breathed a sigh of relief like I always did upon finding her. She was straightening some skulls and other occult items on the shelf. The end of October was the start of the busy season, so I was surprised it wasn't more crowded.

"Bertha?"

She jerked and spun around. "Glinda! I didn't hear you come in. Nice to see you."

I handed her my list of ingredients. "Can you help me with any of these?"

I wish I knew what affect it would have on Nash's and Hunter's healing abilities if I were to obtain all but one of these items.

She studied the list. "What is this for?"

I had rehearsed my spiel. I explained about our deputy being in a fight and that a warlock might have cursed him. I just didn't say with whom he had the fight, or rather with what. "Nash's cuts aren't healing, so I found a spell to reverse this curse."

If she asked how I knew someone had put a curse upon him in the first place, I wasn't sure I could come up with a good answer.

"Let me look."

Phew. I appreciated her discretion. Of the fifteen items on the list, Bertha found three from the shelves located right behind the main desk.

"I have more obscure items in the back," she said.

"Okay."

Bertha was able to find four more from her room in back. "The rest you might be able to find in the forest, assuming you know what to look for."

"I have a friend who can help. Thank you." Not having

the time or inclination to answer more questions, I quickly paid and left.

For the next part of this operation, I wanted Jaxson's help. When I headed upstairs, he wasn't in the office, so I called him.

"Jaxson Harrison," he answered, though he knew full well who it was. I suspected he wanted to put a little levity into my life. He knew I'd be stressed.

"Where are you?" I asked.

"In the wine shop."

"I'm up in the office, but I need to gather some ingredients from the woods for the curse, and I don't want to go alone."

"We'll be right there."

We? A moment later, Jaxson climbed up the interior stairwell with none other than Iggy on his shoulder. "Iggy, have you changed allegiances?" I asked him.

"What do you mean?"

I was surprised he knew the word. "It seems as if you prefer Jaxson to me."

"I like you both equally."

I chuckled at that line. I hoped he was kidding. "I need help."

"Tell us," Jaxson said.

I went over everything that happened at the coven meeting, and that Bertha was able to supply half the ingredients. "The other half are in the woods."

"Maybe the lady who works with Hunter can help," Iggy suggested.

"I'm hoping she can. She is a werewolf and might be able

to smell these plants." I certainly couldn't. "The forest is huge, and a wolf would be able to cover a lot more land."

"Aren't you worried our two werewolf assassins might attack Heather?" Jaxson asked.

"They have no beef with her."

Jaxson gave out an exasperated sigh. "We don't know why they kill or maim. Maybe they know that Heather works with Hunter, and that Hunter was Nash's partner at one time."

I groaned. "You might be right. Heather is from Montana and was a member of their clan, but we can't let that stop us."

"Call Steve."

"What can he do?"

Jaxson placed his hands on my shoulders and turned me to face him. "He has a gun. Mind you, if Heather goes deep into the woods, it won't do much good, but he could follow her a little while and fend off any intruders should they decide they want to take her out, too."

What a sick thought, though it was highly possible they might try. Assuming they had done everything I think they had, these men were pure evil. "We have nothing to lose."

"Come on, let's ask him."

Iggy crawled up my leg. "I'm coming. Please?"

There was that very rare word again. "Why do you want to come?"

"I can help Heather gather some of ingredients. Wolves don't have hands."

I looked up at Jaxson. "He has a point."

"Sure. I have faith that Iggy can easily escape two ravenous wolves. He'll just climb a tree, something I don't think they can do."

"I agree."

"I want to stop back at my apartment first to pick up a small backpack to carry the items in."

"Let's do it," Jaxson said.

After I retrieved what I needed from my place, we went across the street to the sheriff's office. With Nash out, I hoped Steve was there instead of out taking care of some other Witch's Cove business. Pearl was at her desk, and a vase of flowers sat on Nash's. My heart ached for him and the staff.

"Oh, Glinda," Pearl said with such sadness I feared she might expire right at her desk. "Nash is not doing well."

"I know, but I might have a way to help him. Is Steve in by any chance?"

"You can help?" Her hope pierced my soul.

"I think so, but I don't have time to explain. Every minute counts."

She nodded. "Go on back. I'll let him know you and Jaxson are here."

We were halfway to his office when Steve opened his door. "Glinda? My grandmother said something about helping?"

"Yes, but we'd like you to come with us."

"Anything."

I waited for him to chastise me for sticking my nose into this case, but he seemed sincere. I went through the reason why I believed Hunter and Nash couldn't heal. "The only thing that makes sense is that these men are warlocks who also happen to be werewolves. They put a curse on Nash and Hunter to prevent them from ever getting better."

"I've never heard of anything like that."

"Me either." I explained about contacting Levy and then

what his coven found out.

"Do you have the ingredients to do this spell?"

I pulled out my list. "Half of them. The rest I'll need from the forest."

He shook his head. "It's not safe. It's where Hunter, Nash, and I believe these men are."

"I know. It's why I thought I'd ask Heather to help find the remaining ingredients, with you by her side, if possible."

"Me?"

"You have a gun," Jaxson chimed in. "We'll be there too, but as you said, since they might attack humans, we'll stay in the car after speaking with Heather."

"I would be able to concentrate better if you two are out of harm's way. We should go now. Ready?" he asked.

I appreciated his decisiveness. "We are."

"Maybe you can call Heather and give her a heads up. She might not want to chance being in the forest if these men are there," Jaxson said. "It's dangerous, and we'd like to know beforehand so we can create an alternative plan."

"Will do." He called Heather who thankfully was willing to do whatever it took to help both men.

If there was some emergency while he was gone, Steve told Pearl to call Misty if his grandmother couldn't reach him. Thankfully, Pearl seemed to understand how important this mission was.

We took two cars to the forest. Twenty minutes later, we pulled in front of Hunter and Heather's office and got out.

"Can I come?" Iggy asked.

"Sure. She'll need to meet you at some point."

The three of us followed Steve inside past the small museum to the office in back. He introduced us, claiming I was this amazing witch, and Heather motioned we take a seat.

As quickly as I could, I outlined the plan. "Mind you, this could be dangerous if these men are out there."

"I will do anything for Hunter and Nash. The problem is that once I find, say these pine needles, I can't put them in a bag. You have a lot of items for me to gather."

I lifted Iggy out of my purse. "That's where this little fellow comes in. This is Iggy. He is my familiar, which means he can talk, read, pick up stuff. He's very smart." I know I would never hear the end of it after all of that praise.

"Your iguana can talk?"

"Yes, Heather," Steve chimed in. "I can't hear him, but those with powers can. He's been invaluable in solving crimes in the past."

Oh, boy. Iggy would be impossible to live with now. "I brought this sack, hoping you can attach it to yourself somehow. Iggy will ride on top. Trust me, he can cling to anything, so you need not worry he'll fly off."

"I'm liking this praise," he said.

"Shh."

"He said something?" she asked.

"Yes." I didn't want to further boost his ego though. "Here is the list. Can you read when you are in your wolf form?"

She smiled. "Yes, but perhaps Iggy can hold it while I'm looking for the item. When I need to know what's next, he can place it on the ground. Can he do that?"

"She has no idea how good I am." Iggy stuck out his chest.

I didn't answer him. "Yes, he can."

She pushed back her chair. "Let's go."

## Chapter Fourteen

JAXSON AND I had been waiting in the car for over two hours with no news from Steve. I wanted to believe that his cell reception was bad deep in the woods, and that his lack of communication wasn't because something had happened to him. If he or Heather had been injured, eventually Iggy would make his way back here.

I kept reminding myself that locating all of those items would take quite a lot of time. The various plants could be spread out for miles, and Heather seemed to be the type to keep looking until she'd found all of the ingredients. Helping her friends was important to her.

"You're worrying again," Jaxson said.

I faced him. "How can you tell?"

"Seriously? You get this little tick above one eye right here." He pointed to the spot on my face where it appeared.

I rubbed the area. "Tension does that to me. What if the wolves found them? Just because these men might not be able to identify other werewolves, it didn't mean a human's scent isn't strong." I probably shouldn't have suggested Steve go along. If anything happened to him, I'd never forgive myself.

"We would have heard a gunshot by now if they'd been attacked."

That was assuming Steve was given the chance to use his gun. "Maybe."

Heather had suggested we drive to a slightly different location than usual, because she thought she could find more items in another part of the forest. It wasn't near the office area, but rather at a remote path entrance.

Jaxson sat up straighter. "Is that them?"

I opened my door to get a better view. "Yes!"

Steve and Heather emerged with Heather thankfully in her human form. On her shoulder sat Iggy. For once our luck had held. I rushed toward them.

Heather held up the bag and smiled. "I think I got everything. Some of these things were a bit tricky to find. It made me realize that I rely too much on my botany app to identify things."

"I understand." Normally, I might have asked her to tell me which plant was which, but it didn't matter. I was to cook everything together. I plucked Iggy off of her shoulder. "How did Iggy do?"

"I want to keep him."

"That's because I'm special," he told me.

"Yes, you are, buddy." I turned to Heather. "I'm glad he helped."

"He more than helped. Iggy was able to grab most of the plants that I could only sniff at. After placing it in the bag, he showed me the list. He might have read me the names, but even my wolf couldn't understand him."

"I'll be sure to give him an extra treat today, and I will buy you a drink for helping. I never could have done this without you."

"My only thanks will be if you help Nash and Hunter."

"I'm going to try."

"You guys take off. I'll make sure Heather returns safely," Steve said. "And good luck. I need Nash."

"I'll do my best."

As soon as Jaxson and I returned to the car, I gave him directions to Dr. Sanchez's house. The next half hour seemed to take forever even though I spent most of it reading and rereading the spell. Was I even pronouncing the ancient words correctly? In the past, I would have stopped at the tea shop and asked Maude to help me say the words correctly, but we didn't have time today. We'd been gone for hours already. I could only hope that Nash was still hanging on.

"There is her house." Relief washed through me that we'd finally arrived.

"Do you want me to wait in the car?" Jaxson asked.

"No! I need the support."

He smiled. "I'll be right by your side then."

Together we rushed up to the front and knocked. Gavin answered the door. "Hey, come in. My mom said you might be able to help Nash and Hunter?" He looked over our shoulders. "Did Rihanna come?"

"No. We haven't been back to the office. I bet she'd like some company, though. I know she's worried about them." She hadn't said that specifically, but I bet it was true. Not only that, I didn't need Gavin around to watch in case I failed.

He smiled. "Let me check with my mom in case she needs me to help."

Help with what? I followed Gavin down the hallway. When I stepped into the room, it smelled more like death than it had before, but I refused to be defeated.

Dr. Sanchez looked up. "Did you get everything you needed?"

"I did."

"What can I do?"

I looked over at Hunter whose eyes were closed. I hoped he was merely resting and not slowly dying, too. "I need to set up and say the spell. That's all."

"Do you want me to stay?"

"Why don't you fix us something to drink?" For the spell saying part, I'd rather have her in another room.

She stood. "Of course."

As soon as the good doctor left, I pulled over an end table, cleared it off, and placed my bowl on top. I then filled it with all of the ingredients.

"Now what?" Jaxson asked.

"I light it. As I recite the spell, the flame will turn from orange to white. When it turns almost colorless, the curse will be gone."

"Have you ever seen a flame do that? Change colors I mean?" he asked.

I really needed to work on my witch skills. "No, but I have to try."

Jaxson placed a hand on my shoulder. "I believe in you, Glinda."

"Me, too," Iggy said. "Can I help?"

Who was this new familiar? Iggy was usually more reserved and self-absorbed. Maybe he just needed to be appreciated for who he could be. "Jaxson, why don't you put Iggy on Nash's bed. I'm hoping whatever magic he possesses can help with Nash's healing."

"Can do."

Jaxson placed Iggy alongside Nash. I was pleased that Iggy didn't try to crawl on our deputy and further injure him.

With my spell in hand, I lit the bowl. The contents burst into flames and then began to smoke. Oh, no! I don't remember Levy or Camila saying that would happen.

Jaxson rushed over. "Glinda?"

"I didn't think it would do that."

"Try reading the spell, and I'll watch that the room doesn't fill up with too much smoke."

"How about opening the window?" I didn't need the alarm to go off, assuming there was one in here.

While Jaxson took care of that, I recited the spell. "Absolutum dominos creator, bellum totales." I coughed and fanned the burning items. This wasn't going to work.

Suddenly, the hazy mist seemed to morph into what looked like an entity. I blinked a few times. Surely, I was imagining things. "Nana?" I whispered, not wanting Jaxson to think I was hallucinating.

Even though I'd seen my grandmother in her ghost form a few times, I didn't think she'd appear without being summoned—assuming this was her ghost.

"Stop feeling sorry for yourself, Glinda. Finish the chant." Her tone was a bit harsh, and I wanted to deny her charges, but she disappeared before I could say anything. Why did she leave like that? I needed to ask her questions. She was a rather powerful witch and might be able to make some suggestions.

Jaxson placed a hand on my shoulders. "Glinda, what's wrong?"

I was falling apart. "Nothing."

As quickly as I could, I finished the spell, not chastising myself this time for probably mispronouncing the words. When I finished, the flames slowly died down, but they didn't turn white as Camila had said they should.

I'd failed.

Dr. Sanchez came in carrying two glasses. With the door open, the flames immediately jumped back into action, almost as if the cross ventilation gave them the needed oxygen. My pulse shot up. In one glorious Phoenix like resurrection, a beam of white light rose from the bowl's center and then became colorless. Tears trickled down my cheeks. Had I done it? Had I broken the curse?

I swiped away the dampness. Even if these men hadn't been cursed, I didn't know how long it would take for their wounds to heal.

The good doctor handed me some water. "Drink this. I'll check on Nash and Hunter."

I clasped the glass and chugged it down. Nothing could have tasted better. Jaxson took his drink and then gathered Iggy. Who knows? His energy might have helped Nash. "Do you think it worked?" he asked.

"You saw the white light, right?" Maybe I was hallucinating.

"Yes, Glinda, I did."

The doctor checked them out, but so far, I didn't see any improvement. Being patient wasn't one of my strengths. "Anything?" I asked her.

"Nash's breathing seems a little better, and his color is improving a bit."

"Really?"

She turned around and smiled. "I'm hopeful."

Because I had done all I could, it was time to let the good doctor do what she did best. "Thanks for letting me try this."

"No, thank you."

"We'll see ourselves out," Jaxson said.

The doctor stepped over to Hunter. As soon as she placed a hand on his forehead, probably to test his temperature, he opened his eyes.

I rushed over to him. "Hunter?"

"Glinda? Did you get what you needed?"

"I did."

He reached out his hand, and I squeezed it. "Thank you," he said.

"You bet. Rest please."

"Is that it?" Jaxson asked as quietly as he could.

"I don't know, but I think so."

Not wanting to tax Hunter further, Jaxson, Iggy, and I left. I don't know if I had really succeeded or not, but I, too, was hopeful.

Jax smiled. "Good job, witch Goodall."

I chuckled. "After they both heal, I hope they can still shift if they want to. One never knows what side effects can occur with these kinds of spells."

He started the engine. "I'm sure they won't care as long as they are alive."

I wanted to call Steve, but I wasn't sure what I could tell him. Even I wasn't positive the curse had been lifted.

"Let me drop this stuff off back home." I saw no need to go back to the office right now. A nap was calling my name.

"Sure."

Once home, Jaxson parked and then insisted on helping me carry the bowl and bag upstairs, something I could have handled by myself. As we reached the top of the steps, Aunt Fern's door opened, but instead of my aunt coming out, it was our sheriff.

"Steve? What's going on?"

There could have been any number of reasons for him being there.

"I found out some disturbing news and needed more information from your aunt."

I stilled. "What kind of news?"

"Can we go inside your place?"

He sounded ominous. "Sure."

We piled into my place. Jaxson set down my things and headed toward the kitchen. "Tea, anyone?" Jaxson asked.

He understood me so well. "Yes, please."

Steve waved him off. "I'm good."

Once we were seated, my curiosity peaked. "What's going on?"

"You first," he said. "How are Nash and Hunter?"

"It's too soon to tell, but I think better." I explained the process, and then how the white light finally manifested itself. I decided to leave out the appearance of my grandmother's ghost since I thought she might have been a figment of my imagination.

"I'll stop over there as soon as I tell you what I found out."

"What's that?"

"It is my job as sheriff to let the next of kin know of a

loved one's death."

"You contacted Peter's sons?"

Jaxson returned with two drinks and a plate of greens for Iggy. He deserved them.

"I finally managed to reach Peter Upton's oldest son. Apparently, his whole family had been on a cruise for the last month."

"How sad to come home to bad news."

"That's the thing," Steve said. "His *whole* family included his father, Peter Upton."

He wasn't making any sense. "I don't understand."

"The man who dated your aunt and who called himself Peter Upton from White Plains, New York with two sons named Adam and Josh isn't the real Peter Upton. Your aunt's boyfriend stole that man's identity."

My chest caved. "Are you sure?"

"Yes. I compared our dead man's face to the Peter Upton from White Plains, and they are not the same man."

I can't believe Aunt Fern had been duped. "Could there be two Peter Uptons?"

"I had thought that, but would both Peter Upton's have the same address?"

My mind spun. "Then who was he?"

"I haven't run his prints yet. I did go to Upton's office to see if his secretary could offer some help, but she's gone."

"Gone?"

"Yes. The whole office has been cleaned out. No computers or anything. I asked the offices next to his, and they told me she'd just vanished."

"That is really strange." My poor aunt. "I don't know

what to say."

"The best thing you can do is to make sure your aunt is okay. She seemed rather upset."

"Of course, she would be. Lying is the worst offense."

Steve stood. "Thanks for trying to help Nash and Hunter."

"Of course."

With that, he left.

Jaxson slipped next to me. "Do you want to talk to your aunt?"

"I guess I should, but I'm so confused. Who was this guy, and why would he come to Witch's Cove of all places?"

"Learn the answers to those questions, and we might solve this mystery once and for all."

## Chapter Fifteen

I KNOCKED ON Aunt Fern's door and then entered. She was standing by the window, looking out at the ocean, apparently deep in thought. "Aunt Fern?" I tried to be as unobtrusive as possible.

She swiped a finger under her lids and turned around. "You heard, I guess."

I nodded, walked over to her, and then enfolded her in an embrace. "I'm sorry."

"I should have known. He was so good-looking and successful."

I could see where this was headed. "Stop right there. He was lucky to be with you. If he wanted a cover for being here, he could have picked anyone, but he chose you."

"I suppose." She briefly smiled. "We did have fun."

"There you go. That's all that matters." I was going to say she was better off without him, but she might not take it well. I led her over to the sofa. "Can you think of a reason why he would have borrowed another man's identity?"

"He had to have been running from someone. He must have been a criminal."

I tended to agree, but we had no facts. "Steve is still looking into who he really was. Once we learn that, we might know why he was here."

She sniffled. "Thanks. I have figured out one thing. I'm never dating again."

I wrapped an arm around her shoulder. "I've said that a million times myself, but then I'd meet someone else and give in."

"Like Jaxson?"

I had yet to admit where I saw our future going, but I wanted to give her hope that there was someone out that for her. "Yes, like Jaxson."

"I'm happy for you."

"Thanks." I wasn't sure what else I could say to make things better. My aunt needed some time to absorb this news. I was sure that Aimee would be chiming in, but when I looked around, I didn't see her. "Where is that pretty cat of yours?"

"I honestly don't know, but she doesn't stay out too long."

"She might have some insight."

Aunt Fern chuckled. "We'll see."

I stood. "Jaxson is waiting for me, but you know where I am at night. Come over any time you want to talk."

"I will." My aunt stood. "Be careful out there. This whole mess is not over."

"I know." I hugged her goodbye and then walked across the hall to my place.

Jaxson was watching TV with Iggy. "How did it go?" he asked.

"As well as can be expected. She's upset that she was duped. I'm hoping this makes his death easier to take."

"I take it she had no idea who he was?"

"No."

"I doubt his identity will remain a secret for very long. Steve will get his fingerprints and put them in some database. If this guy is a criminal, he should show up somewhere."

"I agree. I hope he's not a horrible person."

Jaxson studied me for a moment. "Because that will make your aunt think she lacks the ability to read people?"

"Yes."

"I get it. I do." Jaxson stood. "I need to head back to the office."

I showed him to the door. I appreciated that he wanted to keep Rihanna safe, but I needed him, too. I wrapped my arms around his waist and pressed my cheek to his chest. "Thanks for coming with me to the forest. I don't think I could have done it by myself."

He leaned back and lifted my chin. "Of course."

Because those men were still out there, I let Jaxson go. I spent the rest of the afternoon and evening reading, but my mind refused to stop going over all of the clues. My biggest issue was who was the fake Peter Upton and was he involved in any way with the other three men? If my arrival dates were right, my aunt's boyfriend arrived in Witch's Cove a few weeks before the other men. Coincidence or planned? What was really bothering me was whether this guy was a werewolf? If he could cloak himself, no one would know if he was one or not, and he certainly wouldn't have confided that tidbit of information to my aunt. I could only hope his prints came up in the system.

As I was heading off to bed, my cell rang. I rushed out to the living room to answer it. "Hey, Hunter. How are you?"

"Doing a lot better, thanks to you."

Hearing his voice bolstered my energy. "That's fantastic. I take it your wolf is healing you?"

"Absolutely."

"And Nash?" I held my breath.

"Why don't you ask him yourself?"

"Really?" I honestly didn't think breaking the curse had worked, let alone work this fast.

"Glinda?" It seemed as if our deputy might not be out of the woods—no pun intended—because he sounded weak, but at least he was alive.

"I'm glad to hear you are on the mend."

"It will take a while. I just want to say… keep up the good work."

Even those few words seemed to tire him out. "Get some rest. Don't worry about a thing. Steve has everything under control."

"Thanks."

"I should be going home tomorrow," Hunter said after taking back the phone.

"I'm sure Penny is worried about you."

"About that. I told her I was out of town on a case. I hope you didn't say anything."

I'd been too busy to talk to her. "No, I haven't."

In the background, I could hear Dr. Sanchez say something to Hunter. "Thanks. Gotta go."

"Sleep well."

I spun to face Iggy. "My spell worked."

He sat up. "Thanks to me."

"Without your help, I never would have been able to

perform the spell, so thank you."

He did his little victory dance. If it hadn't been so late, I might have called Levy, but I would do that tomorrow.

EVEN THOUGH HUNTER, or Nash, probably had called Steve to give him the good news, I thought I'd stop over at the station and tell him. First though, I called Levy to thank him for the spell.

"I'm so happy it worked," he said.

"Me, too. Please thank everyone, especially Camila."

"Will do"

I hung up and headed over to the sheriff's office. When I walked in, Pearl was at her desk with a plate of cookies off to the side. "Did you hear the news?" she asked with a big smile on her face.

"That Nash and Hunter will be okay?"

"Yes. I spoke with Hunter last night, and I hear we have you to thank."

"A lot of people helped. Is Steve in?" I didn't want to get into the spell and how I thought I'd seen my grandmother again.

"He sure is but take a cookie. I don't want to be tempted."

I doubt grabbing one cookie from a plateful would help, but I did love my sweets. With my treat in hand, I knocked on his door and then eased it open.

"Glinda, just the person I want to see."

That was a surprise. I slipped onto the chair in front of his desk. "Yes?"

"The lab returned the glove that you found."

I waited for some information about the results, but he didn't add anything. "Did you learn something?"

"Yes. It belonged to Travis Knowlton. There was Peter's blood—or who we thought was Peter Upton—on the glove, as well as some skin cells that belonged to our other dead man, Travis."

"I take it, that's proof enough that Travis killed my aunt's boyfriend?"

"For now. Considering Travis can't be prosecuted, we're not going to pursue it. I'm convinced his two cohorts did him in. I don't know why they killed him, nor do I have absolute proof, but the evidence points to it."

"Evidence? Beside the fact that these men were cleaning out Travis' house, what do you have?"

"Let's say it's more like circumstantial evidence. Yesterday afternoon, I was able to track down Travis' car. Turns out, someone sold it to a kid in Ocean View for almost nothing. Being young, he was a bit out of control and got into a fender bender."

"That's how you learned about the car sale?"

"Yes. The officer in Ocean View called about it since Travis lived here. Anyway, when I showed this teen the photos of George Fredericks and Tony DeLorenzo, he identified them as the two people who sold him the car."

"Because they were in possession of Travis' car, this sort of proves that these guys killed their friend and were trying to make it look as if he's still alive?"

"That was my thinking," Steve said.

The evidence was rather thin. I hope he was trying to find more. "They must have thought that by clawing at his face, we wouldn't be able to identify him."

"That's my guess, too. I have to say, I am surprised Travis didn't have a record. I searched using not only his name, but also using his fingerprints. The guy was clean."

"Since neither Hunter nor Nash saw the faces of the two werewolves who attacked them, we can't be certain it was these men."

"No, but Misty has sent her officers to the forest. They will check all outgoing and incoming cars. So far, the blue truck is still parked at the forest. When she finds them, she'll bring them here for questioning," Steve said.

"Who's to say they won't leave the forest at some other location and hitchhike somewhere?"

"Let's hope that doesn't happen," he said. "In case it does, I've asked other law enforcement agencies to check the border crossings."

"That sounds excellent."

"While I'm certain these men are the werewolves who killed Travis Knowlton and who also attacked Hunter and Nash, I need real proof, and that's where you come in."

Steve had asked for my help before, but twice in a row? "What can I do?"

"For starters, I'd like you to see if maybe one of your psychics can get a reading off the glove."

"We already know that it belonged to Travis and that he killed the fake Peter."

"Yes, but who's to say she won't learn more?"

He made an excellent point. I didn't know much about

psychic visions. "I'll give it a try. Anything else?"

"Yes. If they don't come out of the forest anytime soon, we'll need to find these men. Since you were able to reverse the curse that prevented Hunter and Nash from healing, maybe you can reverse the cloaking spell that prevents other werewolves from sensing their presence?"

The hope in his eyes almost hurt my stomach. "I've asked Gertrude to find such a spell, but I haven't heard back from her yet."

He lifted the plastic bag that contained the glove. "I'm sure she'll come through. Maybe if you give her this, we'll see what she can make out of it. Levy's group might be able to help with the other spell. I know I don't need to stress that we are under a time constraint."

"I'll do my best."

"If I didn't say so before, thank you for helping Nash. I spoke briefly with him this morning, and I think he's going to be okay."

I smiled. "I think so, too."

The more I thought about it, the more convinced I was that my grandmother had helped with the spell. I grabbed the evidence bag and left, but not before snatching one more cookie.

"Wish me luck, Pearl."

"Luck for what?" she asked.

"With everything."

With that cryptic note, I left and headed across the street to see if Gertrude was there. To my delight she was. Since Steve had asked that I have Gertrude do a reading on the glove, I decided to turn the receipt over to the Witch's Cove sheriff's department. I didn't earn enough to pay for everything.

"You have the glove, I see," Gertrude said as soon as I stepped into her office.

"I do." I told her who it belonged to and that Steve believed this man killed Peter Upton. "Did you hear Peter Upton was a fake name?"

"No. Tell me more."

I couldn't tell if she was pulling my leg or not, but I let her know what Steve had said. "Hopefully, the sheriff will learn why he really was down here."

"Your poor aunt. I'll have to stop by and see her."

"I'm sure she'd love that."

I handed her the glove. "You can take it out of the bag if need be."

Gertrude settled herself on the sofa, placed the bag on her lap, and then put the glove on top. Neither of us knew how much blood was on it.

She closed her eyes, and when she began to sway, I had the sense she was either connecting to the owner or trying to find him. A couple of times she shook her head and then grunted. I only hoped this wasn't too much for her.

About a minute later, her shoulders sagged, and then she opened her eyes.

"Well?" I asked.

"I'm not sure. I saw the number four very clearly, but I also saw some kind of pyramid. The top was red and the bottom black and white."

Okay, that was quite out there. "What do you think that means?"

"I honestly have no idea."

## Chapter Sixteen

GERTRUDE JUST HAD a psychic connection with the glove yet didn't know what it meant? That wasn't really helpful. "There were three men who came to the party who were friends, not four."

She shrugged. "I don't know what to tell you. I'm seeing the number four."

Then it dawned on me. Could Peter Upton be part of the group? "Actually, that gave me an idea. Thank you. I don't know what the pyramid has to do with anything, but the number four could mean something."

Gertrude smiled. "I hope it makes sense at some point."

"There is one other thing. Did you find any kind of spell that would reverse a werewolf's ability to be detected? Or maybe it was a witch's spell that gave them the ability to avoid being identified?"

"I did. Actually, Levy's coven unearthed it. The spell doesn't seem to be too difficult to perform, but you'd have to be fairly close to them to do it."

I sagged. "That's what I was afraid of."

"Where are the men now?"

"We believe the two who attacked Hunter and Nash are still hiding in the woods."

"You don't think they'll come out to eat at some point?"

I really needed to learn a bit more about werewolves. "I honestly don't know. I figure they would kill a rabbit or something."

Gertrude stood and retrieved something off of her desk. She handed me the paper. "This is the spell. No potions needed. No candles to light or anything."

"Thank you. I need to figure how I can implement this without being caught. Do you know how long this spell lasts?"

"No."

"I suppose any length of time would be good enough. Thank you."

After we chatted a bit more, I left and paid, making sure to get a receipt. Once I was back at the office, I called Steve to let him know what Gertrude had said.

"I like your idea that our fake Peter Upton might have been part of this gang. The timing of his arrival and their arrival seems to work, but what does the pyramid mean?"

"Gertrude didn't know, and I can't even guess," I said.

"It's very possible that your aunt's friend was a werewolf who was able to cloak his scent. I do think it's possible he was friends with the other three. But if these men are still in the forest, I don't want you going in there. And that's an order."

Sheesh. I wasn't stupid. "Don't worry. I've seen first-hand what wolves can do to flesh. If they figured out I was trying to stop them from hiding, they'd take me out in a heartbeat."

"I'm glad you understand."

"I'm not going to give up, though. I'll find a way."

"Just be safe, Glinda."

Steve sounded quite sincere. "Thanks."

Iggy waddled out from under the sofa. "Maybe I could go into the woods and say the spell. They couldn't catch me."

I almost chuckled, but then I thought better of it. "I wish you could, but I'm not sure you have the magical skills. I will keep you in mind if I can't come up with a better solution." It wouldn't hurt if he went, but there were dangers in the woods that I didn't want to expose him to.

He stared at me for a bit, probably unsure of whether to be insulted or not. "Okay."

"Where's Jaxson, by the way?" I asked.

"He left you a note. It's on your desk."

Jaxson probably instructed Iggy to tell me right away. Withholding information was his way of being passive aggressive. I went over to my desk. The note said that he was running errands for Drake and would be back in a few hours.

I grabbed an iced tea and plopped down on the sofa, trying to figure out who might be able to get close to these werewolves who was also a witch or warlock. I thought of Camila, the woman in Levy's council, but she wouldn't be safe if they caught on to what she was doing.

No, we needed a way to get these men out of the woods. An idea formed. I called Steve back.

"Glinda? You figured something out I take it?"

I explained that the only way to do the spell would be if these men were free to leave the forest. "I'm all in favor of keeping a roadblock at the border, but it would be great if they could come to town for something. I would prefer a public place where I can casually get close to them."

I crossed my fingers, hoping he would be okay with this plan. My last few plans, harebrained though they might have been, had still worked.

"Like you did with those thieves who broke into the houses and cracked the safes?"

"Exactly."

"I can do that. I'll have Misty remove the patrol cars, but I'll ask her to have one or two men in plain clothes follow them in unmarked cars should they leave. If they come to Witch's Cove or any one of the surrounding towns, I'll let you know."

"You are the best."

"I will be only if this plan works."

I had to laugh. "You know my track record. Anything could happen."

"Later."

When Steve hung up, I felt one hundred percent better.

Even though the spell was easy to understand, the short ones were often the ones where one wrong word could mess up everything. Reading and rereading the spell until I'd committed it to memory seemed to be the best course of action.

In no time, Rihanna came home. "How did school go?" I asked.

She shrugged. "Boring."

That wasn't good. "I thought you liked the new photo teacher."

"I do, but I'd rather be with Gavin or out solving a crime."

Uh-oh, I had a feeling we'd be adding another sleuth to our family in the future. "I might have some work for you."

She perked up. "What is it?"

I explained about the possible chance of *running into* these werewolves in town. "Steve will call us when the men leave the forest and then tell us where they are."

"What if they return to their homes?" she asked.

"I'm not sure. Gertrude said I needed to be close to these men, but how close? I really don't want to sneak around their houses and hope they don't see me."

She snapped her fingers. "I got it. We need them to see Nash to prove that he isn't dead. That way they will hang out around Witch's Cove."

I smiled. "Aren't you the smart one. Let's hope these men would never shift in public."

"Why don't you call Hunter and pass it by him? He might have an idea how to go about it."

"Good thinking." In a way, I was glad that Jaxson wasn't here. He'd be having a fit. "I'll give him a call. He said he was planning on going home today, so hopefully I won't be disturbing him." I called him, and he answered right away.

"What's up, Glinda?"

I explained about having the spell that in theory would cancel George and Tony's ability to hide their werewolf scent and then about Steve's willingness to let the men leave the forest without anyone stopping them. "The problem is I need to be close to them in order to do the spell. I was thinking these men won't want to leave town if they think Nash is alive."

"Are you asking if he is willing to prance down the street or something waving his arms to let everyone know he's okay?"

That gave me an idea. "He's not fit enough for that, but

what if he sits at the Bubbling Cauldron for a while? We could ask Miriam and her posse to spread the word that Nash is alive and well. He's been ordered to take it easy and popped in to her coffee shop."

Hunter whistled. "That sounds a little chancy."

"You and Heather could station yourself close by."

"Heather is in Montana trying to figure out who these guys are."

That was good and not good. Hunter couldn't protect Nash against two wolves should they choose to shift. "I'll think of another plan."

"I didn't say no, yet. What was your original plan?"

I explained about Rihanna and I being in the shop. "If the men came in, I'd say the spell and be on my way. If Rihanna can hear their thoughts, it would be a bonus."

"How will you get the word to them in the first place? I don't sense that they are the type to be in Miriam or Maude's social circle."

Even though his comment sounded humorous, he was right. "That is the sticking point. If enough people are talking about Nash's remarkable recovery, these two werewolves are sure to hear about it. I hope."

"Let me talk to Nash and Steve and see what they think."

"Thank you." I disconnected.

"Well?" she asked.

"Well, what? You didn't read my mind?"

"Glinda, at the moment, your thoughts are so jumbled not even ten psychics could tell what you're thinking."

I laughed. "At least now I know the secret to blocking you." I explained what he said.

"Why don't we grab a cup of coffee now? If Sheriff Rocker calls and changes the location, that works, too. I've been jonesing for some coffee all day."

I smiled. "I could use some myself."

Iggy was at my feet in seconds. "I want to come."

"Why?"

"To give you moral support."

"Speaking of moral support, I'll have to tell Jaxson, so he knows what's going on."

"He'll be mad."

"If there was any other way, I'd do it. I'll say you and I are grabbing some coffee."

"Lying by omission is lying," Rihanna said.

Who was this girl? "I'll say I got the spell and am working on finding a way to execute it."

She smiled. "That will get his attention."

I wrote the note and placed it on his computer. Once I gathered Iggy, the three of us left for the coffee shop. I figured it could be hours before anything happened, but I had nothing else to do.

We'd been seated only a few minutes when Steve called. "Yes, Sheriff Rocker?"

He chuckled. "You are something else."

"What did I do?"

"Your plan might work—at least Nash wants to try. I'll be close by, as will Hunter. I've told my grandmother to start the rumor tree going. No guarantees that these men will hear about Nash being alive and show up in town today or even tomorrow."

"I understand. And thank you."

"No, thank you. If this works, I might have to make you an honorary member of our department."

He was kidding, but I'd love it if it were true. "I appreciate the thought."

We ordered our drinks and a few cookies. I slipped the paper out of my pocket, ready to read it should the need arise.

"Will you recognize them?" Rihanna asked.

"It will be hard to miss a tall bald man and a shorter man with scraggly red hair. Besides, your photos were wonderful." I'd gotten a good look at their faces.

She smiled. "Just checking that you were paying attention."

Miriam came over and looked around. "I hear my place is going to be ground zero for a sting operation."

She was loving this. "I'm hoping so, but our two guests might not learn about it for a while."

Miriam grinned. "It's exciting anyway. I know you'll be here for a while, so coffee refills are on the house."

"You are too sweet. Thank you."

Rihanna and I talked more about Gavin, school, and her plans for next year. When the bell above the door rang, I almost shouted when I spotted Nash, who I had to say was looking so much better than the last time I saw him. He nodded in my direction and then took a seat on the other side of the shop. Should Fredericks and DeLorenzo show up here, I'm guessing he didn't want these men knowing we were friends. That was okay. I was just happy he looked so healthy.

Rihanna leaned forward. "It looks like everyone is on board with this. Do you want to practice reading the spell to me?"

"Sure. The only werewolf in here is Nash, and I don't think his identity is a secret to these men." I picked up the paper and very softly read the spell to her.

"Good job."

I looked at Nash, but he didn't act as if the spell had affected him, which made sense since he hadn't cloaked himself.

My cell rang. It was Steve again. "Yes?"

"Misty called to say Frederick's blue truck left the forest and is heading to town."

"Do you think they learned that Nash is at the coffee shop?"

"I have no idea, but I won't underestimate my grandmother and her friends."

"Amen." When he disconnected, I turned to Rihanna. "We're set to go. All we need is for the men to learn that Nash is here."

"How will they do that?"

I shrugged. "Word of mouth can be powerful."

Fifteen minutes later, Nash left the coffee shop, looking a little weak, but a far cry better from where he was before. I had no idea where he was going, and I wasn't about to ask him. The fact that the sheriff's office was next door might encourage the men to come here in order to watch for a Nash sighting.

Even though I was coffee-logged and stuffed from eating too much, I was determined to see this through. Jaxson had returned to the office and called a few times to make sure I was okay. I caved and explained my plan. To my surprise, he wasn't as angry as I thought he'd be. I'd asked him not to

THE PINK PUMPKIN PARTY

come because the men would surely recognize me if they saw us together, and he actually agreed.

On Jaxson's last call, he said he was heading over to the sheriff's office just in case Steve needed help.

It was around dinner time when the coffee shop doors opened. Just as I was about to check out the newcomer, Rihanna kicked me under the table.

I looked up. "What?"

When I spotted our two subjects at the counter, I nearly froze. "That's them," I whispered, forgetting that I probably didn't need to say that. Rihanna knew who they were.

"Say the spell," she mouthed.

Sheesh. I'd practiced until I'd memorized the thing, but I took out the paper anyway. Tilting my head to the side to make sure they didn't catch sight of my face, I repeated the spell. Gertrude never said what would happen after that, but I figured it would be up to Nash and Hunter to let me know if I'd been successful.

Rihanna pushed back her chair. "Give me your credit card so I can pay."

The refills might have been on the house, but not all of the food I'd consumed. I slipped it out of my purse and handed it to her. I was guessing her goal was to get close enough to these men in order to either hear what they were saying, or to read their minds. Either way worked for me.

When I watched her go up, I was struck dumb by one very, very strange image.

## Chapter Seventeen

WHAT THE HECK was going on? The two men at the counter were glowing yellow. I'd never seen anything like it before. I checked the rest of the room, but no one seemed to have noticed. Even Rihanna was acting as if everything was normal. Maybe my imagination had gone wild. After all, I thought I'd seen my grandmother when I was doing the last spell.

A few seconds later, Rihanna returned to the table. "I paid. We need to leave," she whispered.

The stress in her voice convinced me it was time to go. "Okay."

After making sure Iggy was tucked away tight in my purse, we left. I motioned we inform the sheriff what had gone down. Only after I stepped inside the safety of the office did my pulse slow.

"Why were they glowing yellow?" Rihanna asked, her brows pinched.

My muscles almost melted. "Thank goodness you could see that."

"Granted, it didn't seem as if anyone else noticed. Even the two men had no idea, and I could tell what they were thinking."

Pearl wasn't at her station, so we went straight back to Steve's office. I could hear Jaxson and Nash chatting in the room. I knocked and then we stepped inside. "The two men are at the coffee shop," I announced.

"I know," Steve said. "I have spies stationed everywhere."

Nash turned around. "Did you put the spell on them?"

"Yes, but I might have messed up. They are glowing yellow, and I don't think that is supposed to happen."

"Yellow?" Nash asked.

"Yes, yellow. I could see it, as could Rihanna, but no one else seemed to notice."

Nash pushed back his chair. "In case they are still there, I want to see if I can sense them."

"Don't go!" Rihanna nearly shouted.

Nash eased back down. "Why?"

"I was standing next to them, and they were quite angry that you were still alive. The bald one kept blaming the red-headed man for the mistake, saying that he'd been the one to mess up."

"Then I will be careful. I won't go inside, assuming they are still there."

Steve shook his head. "Let me ask Hunter to check it out."

He pulled out his phone and dialed Hunter's number. After a brief explanation, he hung up. "Now we wait."

Sometimes this job was frustrating.

"Glinda has done her job," Steve said. "We now can find these men, maybe easier than I thought." He smiled. "Hey, maybe they'll glow in the dark."

That would be funny. "That only helps if you can see

them. No one else seemed to notice."

The front door to the office opened, and a few seconds later, Hunter walked in. Steve stood. "How about we move to the conference room? It's a bit crowded in here."

Before we'd had the chance to sit down in the new location, Hunter announced that the two men were on the move.

"Could you tell they were werewolves," I asked, with quite a lot of pride in my voice.

Hunter's brows pinched. "No, was I supposed to?"

"You didn't see their yellow glow?" Rihanna asked.

"Yellow glow?"

Darn it. Once more I explained about the spell, and how it was designed to reverse it. "I figured when they started to glow, it meant they could no longer hide."

"Did Gertrude tell you this would happen?" Steve asked.

"No. All she said was the spell would be reversed. I assumed that meant other werewolves could now detect them. I never expected the color thing." Heck, I wasn't sure I had reversed anything.

Hunter sat next to me and ran a hand down my arm. "It was a good try."

"We can't give up now," I said. "We strongly believe these guys murdered Travis Knowlton and that Travis murdered the fake Peter Upton. These men need to be brought to justice."

"I agree," Hunter said.

"Do you know where they are headed?" Steve asked.

"Misty's people are following them. She'll let us know if they return to the forest or go back to their house."

"They might leave town," Jaxson said.

"Not without making sure Nash is dead," Rihanna said.

"They'll need time to regroup. They planned the first attack, but now they'll need another one."

Everyone sat up. "How do they know he's alive?" I asked. "Nash wasn't in the coffee shop when they came in. We can't be positive they will fall for hearsay."

"I didn't get a chance to tell you, but when I was up at the counter standing next to these men, Miriam was there. I motioned with my eyes that these were the guys we were after." She smiled. "Miriam is sharp. Our gossip queen came over and announced that I'd just missed Nash, that he'd come in for a To-Go order moments before. I could read the men's thoughts. Trust me, they believed her."

"Then we have to do something," I announced.

I looked over at Steve. Surely, he wouldn't let them get away. "Don't even think it, Glinda. I'm not having you lead us into the woods—assuming they go back there—just so we can arrest them. They'll have to emerge at some point, and when they do, we'll get them."

"They could stay in there for days."

"She has a point," Nash said.

Finally, someone was on my side. "I can find them. They glow, which makes them hard to miss. Once I point them out, I'll leave and let you lawmen take care of them."

"I don't like it," Jaxson said, "but I know once Glinda sets her mind to something, it's hard to change it. I only ask that we have more than just Hunter and a yet-to-be-healed Nash try to take them down."

I reached under the table and squeezed Jaxson's hand.

"Do you two know more werewolves? As in reliable ones who can fight?" I asked.

My father was reliable, but he hadn't been trained to fight. Hunter and Nash looked at each other.

"Other than Heather, no," Hunter said.

As if they'd conjured her up, she appeared at the door. She tapped lightly and then entered. "What did I miss?"

"Welcome, Heather," Steve said. "Heather has been to Montana to hopefully learn who these men are. Any luck?"

She smiled. "A lot of luck." When she spotted Nash, she almost did a double take. "When I spoke with Steve last night, he said that Glinda had been able to reverse the spell, but I didn't expect you to be up and around so soon."

He smiled. "I had a good nurse, and I know a witch." He looked over at me and winked.

That made my day. "Aw, thanks."

"Glinda, why don't you bring Heather up to speed, and then she can hopefully provide us with some valuable intel," Steve said.

I nodded, and then began with my procuring the spell that would allow other werewolves to identify these men. "I don't know what went wrong, but instead of you all being able to smell them, or whatever you do to tell they are werewolves, now only witches can see them—or at least Rihanna and I can see them. I'm assuming all witches can."

"What are we going to do?" Heather asked.

"It's what we are trying to figure out," Steve said. "But tell us your news first."

"Okay. For starters, Danny Wheaton, our current clan leader, thinks he figured out exactly what happened." We all stilled. "Nash, do you remember Preston Gorman?"

"How could I not? He terrorized Mill River and killed

several innocent bystanders."

"Yes, and because you ended his reign of terror, so to speak, his father has been determined ever since to take you down."

Nash looked off to the side. "I don't remember meeting him."

"You may not have. Preston's dad was Duncan Gorman, aka Peter Upton."

The room burst into conversation. We bombarded Heather with so many questions at once that Steve had to bang the table. "Let Heather finish."

"Thanks. Duncan recruited your three amigos: Travis, George, and Tony."

Nash shook his head. "I know Preston was in a different clan, but I don't remember these guys."

"I imagine they were stray punks that Duncan picked up after we all moved down here." She held up a hand. "I take that back. Travis was his second in command. The other two were hired hands."

"Do you think Travis killed this Duncan leader so he could be in charge?" I asked.

She shrugged. "We might never know unless George or Tony talk."

"For that to happen, they need to be caught," I tossed out.

The image of the pyramid popped into my head. "This might sound crazy, but Gertrude received an image from the Spiderman glove that Travis dropped outside of the party. She saw the number four as well as a pyramid. Could this pyramid be the hierarchy of the clan, with this Duncan guy on top and

Travis underneath?"

Everyone looked at Nash. "It is certainly possible. It might explain why Travis killed Duncan."

"Why kill Travis?" I asked.

Nash shrugged. "Take out the number two man so whoever is left is now in charge?"

That sounds like the last werewolf clan that came through here. "That would make George or Tony the Clan leader, assuming those back home don't rebel."

"I'm glad Hunter and I aren't up there anymore to see that play out," Nash said.

"That begs the question, how can we catch the two remaining werewolves?" Steve asked.

"That is where our old clan members come in," Heather said.

"What do you mean?" Steve asked.

"When I told them what had happened to Nash and Hunter, they rallied. About ten will be here on a later flight tonight to track down these men."

My pulse soared. "As in ten more werewolves?"

Yes, that was a dumb question considering she'd just told me they were clan members, but I was too excited to think straight.

Heather chuckled. "Yes."

I sagged in relief. "If I can find them, then you all can take them down—or rather those who can shift can take them down."

Jaxson squeezed my thigh, probably to indicate he was happy I wasn't insisting that I be the one to charge into danger—as if I would.

Steve's cell pinged. He read what was on the screen. "That was Misty. Our two suspects just entered the forest after stopping at the grocery store."

"It would be easier to escape if you could hide in a few thousand acres," Hunter offered. "They have to know we're on to them, which is why they aren't returning to their homes."

Steve nodded. "Let's come up with a plan to get these guys once and for all." He held up a hand. "I realize that if these men decide to shift that I will not be the one to stop them."

"Are we to assume we have the authority to bring them in dead or alive?" Hunter asked.

"You know I'd love it if they didn't resist, but I doubt that will be the case. I want them to stand trial, but I fear it might be hard to prove that they attacked you and Nash even if we try them in a court of their peers."

"That's true," Nash said. "It would be their word against ours. We're pretty sure Travis killed his boss, the man we know as Peter Upton."

"That is easier to prove," Steve said. "Though it doesn't matter much now since Travis is dead. All we can arrest them for is killing Travis or harming you two."

"Can you prove they killed Travis?" I asked. "Packing up their friend's possessions and selling his car would do it for me if I were on a jury."

"I hope you're right, Glinda." Steve placed his palms on the table. "I guess you all know what that means." He looked over at Heather. "Will the men from your clan be here and ready to go by nine?"

She smiled. "You can count on it."

## Chapter Eighteen

"I STILL DON'T know why I can't go," Rihanna said. "We're the only two who can see these werewolves."

"You're right, but I couldn't live with myself if anything happened to you," I shot back.

"Happened to me? If those wolves see us and attack, there will be at least five other highly trained werewolves to take them down. And if that fails, I won't be the one they eat."

My eyes widened. "Are you saying they'd eat me first?"

Rihanna huffed. "Ah, yeah. I can run twice as fast as you, and that is all that matters."

"Ladies, ladies. Enough of this bickering," Jaxson said. "I think Rihanna might be right. It's possible we'll need to divide and conquer. There should be enough of Nash's clan there to protect both of you, but only if we stick together at first."

I looked over at Jaxson to see if he was trying to appease Rihanna or if he really meant it. He was the cautious one of the group. "Fine, but you go rogue even one time, and I won't be able to trust you again."

Rihanna smiled and then crossed her heart. "I promise I won't."

Iggy hopped up on the table. "Don't even think about leaving me behind."

There was no way I was taking him. He'd go off on his own and possibly put the group in jeopardy by having to look for him. "Someone needs to stay back and watch Nash's back."

"He's not going?" Iggy asked.

"No. It's what the two men want—to get him alone. Actually, one of the clan members will stay back at the station just in case they come in. Steve suggested that Nash take a nice nap in one of the empty jail cells with the door locked. He'd be safe until Nash's bodyguard can take care of the men."

Iggy looked between all three of us. "Isn't he upset that he's not going?"

"Very, but he's not ready." I snapped my fingers. "You could wait at the door. If anyone sneaks in, you could cloak yourself, race to the cell, and let Nash know they were there."

"He can't hear me."

"I know, but if you jump on him, he'll know something is up. It's a very important role."

"Fine," he said. "You own me a big plate of greens though."

I smiled. "The biggest."

Jaxson tapped his watch. "It's time."

Once back at the office, we dressed. Both Rihanna and I slathered on the green face paint to make us more invisible. I had gone against my rules once more by wearing my dark jeans, but even I realized that pink kind of glowed in the dark. After Rihanna lent me one of her black shirts and black cap to cover my hair, I was all set.

As soon as she emerged, I sucked in a breath. "No one will

see you."

"That's the point." She picked up Iggy. "Ready?"

Our first stop was the sheriff's office to drop off Iggy. "He'll make sure Nash is awoken if anyone enters the station." I turned to our deputy. "Don't worry, Iggy will be gentle."

He smiled. "I will feel very safe now that he's here."

"Remember, he can cloak himself, so if you don't see him, it doesn't mean he's not there."

"Got it."

The stationhouse was packed with very large men I didn't know. Being surrounded by so many werewolves was a bit daunting. I was glad that they didn't glow yellow.

Steve introduced both of us. "These ladies can see these men glow, if that's the right term."

"Good enough," I said. "I'm hoping the spell is still holding."

Rihanna leaned over. "Do you still have the spell?"

I tapped my forehead. "It's all up here. Trust me. I won't be forgetting it anytime soon."

"All right, men and ladies," Steve said. "You all know your assignments. Chris, Thad, and Randy are assigned to the ladies here. Surround them, and we'll be good. Ready?"

The group agreed in unison. Jaxson drove Rihanna and me, while Chris, Thad, and Randy followed closely behind. We'd been assigned to the Picket Post Path parking lot area since that was near where the fight with Hunter and Nash had occurred. If these men suspected the cops were on to them, they'd probably move pretty far into the woods. It was why I was wearing my small backpack with a few bottles of water and some snacks. I had no idea how many miles we'd have to travel.

When we arrived, my nerves flared. "Who's to say these guys didn't call in more reinforcements," I asked to no one in particular.

Chris stepped next to me. "We have people monitoring that. We'll know if they hop on a plane to come down here. Don't worry. We're not going to let anyone get near Nash—or Hunter, for that matter. The clan is our family."

Aw. It almost made me wish I was a werewolf. Okay, not really. I had enough to handle being a witch.

Thad motioned toward the trail. "Chris and I will lead, and Randy will take up the rear. Any questions?"

We all said no.

As we headed into the dark forest, I bet Jaxson wished he still had the ability to see in the dark, like he could after I put that spell on him. Because it was so dark, I figured it would be easy to spot these men, assuming they were still glowing yellow. Now, I was glad that I'd let Rihanna talk me into letting her come with us. It was hard to look in every direction.

"They could be in tents," Rihanna whispered.

"Shh. I don't need that kind of negativity. We have to think positively, or we won't find them. This forest is really huge."

We weren't the only group who was searching. Steve said he was hoping these men would get cocky and light a fire, which would be nice.

After two hours of walking the trail, my feet hurt. At least Florida was a flat state. If I had to climb a mountain, I would have given up a long time ago. The worst part was that Chris instructed us not to talk.

I was dreaming of a nice long soak in a tub, when a flash of light off to the side caught my attention. I stopped, and Rihanna nearly bumped into me.

"Watch it," she whispered.

Not wanting our voices to carry, I turned her toward the light. The men in front must have heard us, because they stopped. I pointed to the yellow glow about two hundred feet through the woods.

"I see it, too," Rihanna said, sounding excited.

Was this it? The moment we were waiting for?

"Thad and I will check it out," Chris said softly. "Randy, stay with them, but text Steve just in case these are the guys."

Calls were a bit sketchy to connect, but texts always went through, or so we were told.

The three of us watched, but I couldn't really see anything. I especially couldn't see Chris or Thad. They moved so quietly, I began to wonder what they were doing.

Randy's phone lit up, and he pressed the screen close to his chest. "It's the men. Time for us to go."

I wanted to watch. Surely, Chris and Thad could handle these guys, right? Then a howl pierced the still night, and Jaxson tugged on my arm.

"Glinda!" he whispered.

Part of me wanted to run—though if I did, I'd probably trip—and the other part wanted to watch. I'd never seen wolves fight. Because it was so dark, I might not see much though. George and Tony still glowed even in their wolf form.

Randy ushered the three of us down the path. While I didn't relish a two-hour hike back, I was more relaxed knowing we were safe.

By the time we reached the car, my legs were like jelly. After thanking Randy for his guidance, I had to practically crawl into the car. I promised myself that I would walk the beach every day to get in shape. Whether that would happen was anyone's guess.

When we arrived at home, I said I needed a shower. Bad. "Then I'd like to grab something to eat."

Rihanna smiled. "When aren't you hungry?"

"Never?"

"Rihanna and I will shower at the office and then come pick you up. What will it be? The Tiki Hut or the diner?"

"The Tiki Hut. I want to bring my aunt up to speed on what happened."

Jaxson smiled. "I like my pink lady, green-faced."

"Don't get used to it."

"When I finish showering, I'll head on over to the sheriff's office and pick up Iggy. He'll want to celebrate with us—assuming we hear back from Steve that all went according to plan."

"Great idea. Thank you."

While I cleaned up, I waited for some news from someone in the know. I figured once they returned to town, word would get out about what happened.

It took about forty minutes before Rihanna and Jaxson returned. When they stepped inside, Iggy was riding on Jaxson's shoulders.

"I know something," he said rather smugly.

"Do tell." I would have asked if this could wait until we'd ordered, but I had the sense he did have news I wanted to hear.

"One is dead, and the other is on his way to some place where werewolves who've been bad go," my familiar announced.

"Who is dead? I hope either George Fredericks or Tony DeLorenzo."

"Yes, one of them." Iggy was usually a bit chattier, but at the moment he seemed to be relishing doling out the information bit by bit.

"What about Chris and Thad?"

"I think they are fine. A bit scratched up, but Nash told me that was par for the course. They would heal."

Relief poured off of me. "Does that mean the case is over?"

Jaxson moved close and wrapped his arms around my waist. "It means exactly that. You did it again. You saved the day."

I laughed. "Rihanna, Levy, and Gertrude all had a hand in this, too." Iggy tilted his head. "And Iggy and you, too. It was a team effort."

"I wonder if the day will come when we help bring down the bad guy and get paid."

"I think we are destined to be poor and do pro bono work."

Rihanna cleared her throat. "I thought someone was hungry."

That was my hint to unhook my arms and go downstairs. "Let me knock on Aunt Fern's door. Hopefully, she'll join us."

I locked up and walked across the hall. She must have

heard us, because she opened up before I could knock. "What's going on?"

"We're going to grab something to eat downstairs, because we are celebrating."

She smiled. "I take it the men were caught?"

"Yes. Come on. We'll tell you everything."

My aunt glanced at the ceiling and closed her eyes for a moment, almost as if she was talking to Uncle Harold.

Considering everything that had happened in this case, I was quite confident that he was answering her.

## Chapter Nineteen

WITHIN A WEEK, the Tiki Hut was back to its usual hustle and bustle. Even Aunt Fern seemed to have come to grips with being duped by the man who called himself Peter Upton. As for the original four men determined to take down Nash Solano, only George Fredericks was still alive. Apparently, what had started out as a four-person pyramid was now down to one.

George had recovered from his capture and was awaiting trial in a prison designed for his kind. I say good riddance to him. George confirmed that Travis killed Peter—or rather Duncan Gorman—in order to assume the role of clan leader. Naturally, he said he knew nothing about Travis' plan. And because out-and-out murder of a clan leader was not the way to assume leadership, Tony, and only Tony, took it upon himself to put Travis in his rightful place. George had been unable to explain how there were two sets of claw marks on Travis' body, however.

When questioned about the direct attack in the woods on Nash and Hunter, George denied all guilt. It didn't matter. In this particular court of law, other kinds of evidence would be admissible—like that of Rihanna being able to read their minds. Nash assured everyone that George Fredericks would never walk freely in the light of day again, and that put my mind at ease.

Now I could turn my attention to the next challenge in my life—that of working on the Thanksgiving and then the Christmas decorations at the Tiki Hut. Just because I had another job—at least in theory—that in no way excused my involvement in being the head of the decoration committee. I counted the days until both holidays.

Yikes! I had a lot of presents to buy this year. Iggy was easy. I always ordered some hibiscus leaves from the florist, which he totally loved. My mom usually would send me a link or two to some blouse she'd found online, along with some Wizard of Oz memorabilia she'd located on eBay. That was easy to do, and Mom was always happy with her gifts.

Dad and Aunt Fern were easy to please, too. It would be Rihanna and Jaxson who would be the hardest, but I had time before the panic set in.

I was sitting at my office desk, going through our finances when the door burst open and Rihanna rushed in. Ever since school started, she'd been working with Gertrude and Levy on honing her psychic skills, and her progress—according to her two teachers—was quite remarkable.

"I did it!" she announced.

Iggy, who'd been sleeping under the sofa, peaked his head out. "Did what?"

"I contacted my dad."

Her father had been murdered about six weeks ago, and she'd been a little out of sorts that she never got to talk to him—father to daughter—before he died. Even though his killers had been caught, he'd yet to answer her pleas of speaking with him from the beyond.

"That's amazing. How?"

Rihanna sat down on the sofa. "Gertrude said she might have been able to get him to talk, but that I'd be a lot happier if I had a way to do it by myself."

"By yourself? Like when my Mom talks to the dead?"

"Kind of. I think. I'm sure it helps that I have some genetic inclination toward speaking with those who've passed, but I talked to him in my mind and not with my mouth, if that makes any sense. It takes a lot of concentration, but eventually, I can hear his words. Then we talk, like I'm in some kind of dream. Only I'm not, I'm awake."

I didn't follow all of it, but if she was able to communicate with her dad, I was very happy for her. "I think that's great. I wish Aunt Fern could have that with Uncle Harold. He seems to be the only man who ever treated her right."

I never believed in soul mates, but maybe they did exist.

Rihanna sat up. "Maybe I can help her."

"Help her how? Help her connect with Uncle Harold?"

"Yes."

"He used to come around every day—while in his ghost form—but eventually, he said she should move on."

"He might like lucid dream walking then." Rihanna smiled. "That's what I'm calling it. It won't take much effort for him to appear."

"I think it's wonderful. Why don't you ask her if she'd like to give it a try?"

Rihanna stood. "I will."

My cousin had so much energy.

"While you're at it, if you have any ideas on decorating

the Tiki Hut Grill for Thanksgiving, let me know."

She chuckled. "I have only one request."

"What's that?"

"No more pink pumpkins. And please remember the pilgrims only wore black."

I'm sure they wore a few other colors, but light pink was probably not something the average folk would have access to. "It's a deal, but I'm putting a pink bow on sprigs of mistletoe at Christmas."

She grinned. "And who are you hoping to catch with this sprig of love?"

"Who knows?" Of course, she and I both knew that I only had eyes for Jaxson.

Iggy crawled up on top of the coffee table. "Can I get some catnip mistletoe?"

Eww. "For you and Aimee?"

"Who else?"

I smiled. "I'll see what I can do, but Christmas is six weeks away."

"I know." He crawled down to the floor. "I'm going with Rihanna. I want to learn to conjure my ancestors."

I laughed. "Good luck with that, buddy."

I probably should have taken it more seriously. Iggy had some magical talents, and maybe we hadn't tapped into the spiritual aspect of them yet.

As soon as they left, I went back to work on my finances. Not more than ten minutes later, Jaxson came upstairs from the wine shop.

"Hey," he said. "I've been thinking."

I turned to face him. "About?"

"What do you say we take a break from our busy lives and maybe go parasailing?"

"Parasailing? I've never been." So what if the weather was perfect this time of year, I was a little scared to go up in the air.

His brows rose. "There has to be a first time for everything."

"Why that? And why now?"

He pulled up a chair and sat next to me. Jaxson then lifted my hands into his. "Because I want to spend the day with you. It will be fun. Is that so hard to understand? These last few weeks—no make it these last few months—have been hectic. All we do is work, work, and work. Someone is always needing our services, and I thought it would be nice to put that aside and enjoy ourselves. No Rihanna and no Iggy. Just the two of us." He squeezed my hand. "You do know the word *fun*, right?"

I swallowed a smile. "Not at all, but if you're patient, maybe you can show me?"

He lifted my hands to his lips and kissed them. "It would be my pleasure."

My pulse soared. "Then I say let's do it."

I hope you enjoyed seeing how Glinda, Jaxson, and Rihanna sorted through so many clues. Thank goodness they had a lot of help in unearthing several magic spells to help. In book 8, The Pink Iguana Sleuth company finds themselves in a total quandary. They have been sent back in time and have no idea why. Their big dilemma (besides having to solve a murder) is how to return to the twenty-first century!!

Mistletoe and the Pink Bow (book 8 of A Witch's Cove Mystery) is available.

Buy on Amazon or read for FREE on Kindle Unlimited

*Don't forget to sign up for my Cozy Mystery* newsletter *to learn about my discounts and upcoming releases. If you prefer to only receive notices regarding my releases, follow me on BookBub.*
http://smarturl.it/VellaDayNL
bookbub.com/authors/vella-day

Here is a sneak peek.

"WHAT DO YOU think?" I held up a sprig of mistletoe tied together with a pink bow.

My cousin, Rihanna, laughed. "Where do you plan to put that?"

I shouldn't be surprised she acted as if mistletoe was some old-fashioned tradition. After all, she was just a teenager. I personally thought it was romantic, and yet I was only nine years older than her. "In Jaxson's house. We're spending Christmas Eve there."

"Okay, I'll admit that does sound like fun." Thankfully, she seemed sincere.

"And you? Do you and Gavin have plans?"

My cousin and Gavin Sanchez, an intern at his mother's medical examiner practice, had been dating for about three months. Rihanna was eighteen and technically an adult, so I never questioned her about their relationship. She was a very pretty girl who had turned into a self-confident woman since moving here, and Gavin was bright and focused. I trusted them both.

"He's taking me out to dinner to some place in Ocean View. It's supposed to be quite nice." She smiled and then sighed.

I was happy for her. She'd not had the easiest upbringing. When she moved to Witch's Cove, Florida, from across the state four months ago, she'd been sullen, rebellious, and withdrawn, but I understood why she was unhappy. My aunt had not been a good role model, especially after Rihanna's father disappeared when my cousin was only one-year old. He reemerged sixteen years later, and because of Uncle Travis' sudden appearance, Aunt Tricia decided to go into rehab. From what my mother told me, Rihanna's mom would be released in a few weeks.

What my cousin's next step would be, I wasn't sure, but I didn't want her to leave here, that was for sure. Between myself and Jaxson—and Gavin, of course—I hoped she'd chose to stay until she at least finished her senior year of high school. If she wanted to make Witch's Cove her permanent home after that, I, for one, would be thrilled.

"That sounds wonderful," I said. "Don't forget we are due at my parents' place tomorrow at noon to open some presents and then have Christmas dinner."

"I'll remember, don't worry."

My mom had invited Gavin and his mother, too, since Elissa's in-laws were going out of town. Naturally, I wanted Jaxson to come, but he'd already committed to going back home with his brother, Drake. Because Jaxson's younger brother was the one to visit their parents on a semi-regular basis, Jaxson felt the need to be there at least on Christmas Day. He'd steered clear of his folks for many years due to some bad choices he'd made growing up.

Iggy, my fifteen-year-old pink iguana familiar crawled out from under the sofa wearing a green hoodie, one of the early Christmas presents my Aunt Fern had made for him. Even though we lived in Florida, it could get chilly here, and the office was rather drafty. Being cold-blooded, Iggy needed to stay warm to survive. I had to admit he looked adorable in his spiffy new outfit.

"Christmas is tomorrow. Did you both buy me some presents?" he asked.

I chuckled. "Did you get us anything?" I totally understood it was a ridiculous comment, but I didn't want him to be any more entitled than he already was.

"Maybe."

From the way he averted his gaze, that was a hard no. Footsteps sounded on the interior staircase from the wine and cheese shop below. That would be Jaxson Harrison, my business partner in our new venture, The Pink Iguana Sleuths.

Yes, Iggy's ego soared because of that title.

I smiled, happy every time I saw him. "Hey."

"Ready to grab that bite?" he asked.

"I am." I had already asked Rihanna if she wanted to join us for lunch, but she said she wanted to pick up one more present for Gavin.

Iggy didn't like the cold, so for once he was willing to stay back at the office and keep things under control. What he could do if anyone broke in, I didn't know, but he liked being given the responsibility of office protector.

I grabbed my jacket from the back of the sofa and shrugged it on. It might be sixty-degrees outside, but for this Florida native girl, that was cold. Please don't judge.

Before I get too far into this narrative, let me introduce myself. I'm Glinda Goodall, a twenty-seven-year old former math teacher, who decided that I was better suited to being a waitress than dealing with middle schoolers.

After our first town murder happened, however, Jaxson convinced me I should open this sleuth agency with him, mostly because I'm terminally nosy. I also happen to be a witch, and that particular talent—when my spells actually worked the way they were supposed to—helped solve several crimes. I need to point out that our town is full of psychics, witches, and on occasion, some rogue werewolves. Too often, one needed to fight magic with magic, so to speak.

We were half way to the Tiki Hut Grill when something shiny on the ground caught my attention. Normally, I wasn't the type to pick up a coin, but this particular one was gold-colored, so I bent down and snatched it. Jaxson stopped so we could both look at it. "Have you seen anything like this before?" I asked as I turned it over.

"No. It looks like it came from a game, or else it's some fake doubloon like the ones they toss from balconies or floats during Mardi Gras."

"You're probably right." I was about to drop it when Jaxson grabbed my wrist. "Or it could be wish coin."

I laughed. "A wish coin? What is that?"

"My grandmother used to say that if you find a coin on the road, pick it up, and make a wish. It just might come true."

"Was grandma big into buying lottery tickets, too?"

He laughed. "Turns out, she was."

I had to assume his grandmother never hit it big. "For grandma, I will give it a try." A gust of wind blew off the Gulf and chilled me, forcing me to pull my coat tighter. "How about we get to the restaurant first? Besides, I have to think of a wish. I only get one, right?" I wanted to know the Harrison family rules.

He smiled and wrapped a protective and warm arm around my waist. "Yes, you only get one. Come on."

The Tiki Hut, which was owned and run by my Aunt Fern, was surprisingly busy, but we were seated rather quickly. My aunt, who was standing behind the check-out counter, waved. I figured as soon as she finished with the couple who was paying, she'd stop over for a quick chat. We sat down, and I slipped off my jacket.

"What is your wish?" Jaxson asked.

I thought he might have forgotten about it, but he seemed quite serious. I didn't want to pick any subject too deep—like something that involved us—nor did I want to make light of the situation. I wanted to do the coin justice, which meant I wouldn't say I wanted to have someone hand me a million dollars. That wasn't going to happen, wish or no wish.

I looked outside at the rather grayish day to help me decide. Then inspiration struck, and I turned back to Jaxson. "I have it. When I was a little girl, every Christmas Eve I would ask my parents if they could make it snow on Christmas Day. You see, Mom would play all the Christmas classics, especially those by Bing Crosby and Perry Como. Hearing about a white Christmas made both of us rather sentimental, I guess." I placed my coin in my palm and then closed my fist around it. "My wish is to see snow on Christmas."

Jaxson leaned back in his chair. "You do realize that probably won't happen unless we hop in a car and drive north for about fifteen hours."

He was being silly. "I do realize that, but I read it snowed here back in the seventies. It could happen again."

"The forecast for tomorrow calls for temperatures in the seventies."

I shrugged. "A wish is a wish. Don't forget, I am a witch. Maybe it will come true."

Jaxson reached across the table and squeezed my hand. "Dream on, pink lady."

That nickname *pink lady* came about because I only wore pink. Even I didn't know why I did—genetic defect maybe? I shut my eyes and pretended to conjure snow. That was way, way out of my witch abilities, but a girl's gotta try. When a good ten seconds had passed, I opened my eyes. "I realize I've used up the wish on this coin, but if you had one of your own, what would you wish for?"

"Hmm. That is a hard one."

I couldn't believe I was actually holding my breath. Was I hoping he'd say that we could always be together? That was silly, of course. Our relationship had only just begun.

"My wish is that we have a constant stream of clients for our blossoming business."

His choice didn't surprise me. Of the two of us, Jaxson was the practical one. "I hope that comes true as well."

Once we ordered, my aunt came over. "Do you two lovebirds have plans for tonight?"

Lovebirds? I wanted to disappear. Sure, Jaxson and I were a couple, but so far, we'd kept it fairly simple. "We do. I'm envisioning some popcorn, soft music, and a nice warm fire." And some kissing, of course, which was why I planned to take the mistletoe with me. "What are your plans?"

I know my parents had invited her to spend the evening with them, but so had several of her friends. Even since she'd been betrayed—if that was the right word—by her last boyfriend, Aunt Fern had kept to herself. That was a shame, since she used to have an active social life.

"We're having a girls' afternoon over at Miriam's. We'll each bring a gift and have a mini-Christmas party. We had to do it early because Pearl wants to spend some time with her grandson."

"That sounds fun." From the way her eyes were shining, she was quite excited about it. "Who else will be there?"

"The usual crew: Maude, Pearl, Dolly, and myself."

Of course. The five gossip queens. The Pink Iguana Sleuths might not have solved even one case had it not been for their information. It certainly helped that the eldest member, Pearl, was the sheriff's grandmother who worked as his receptionist, despite the fact her hearing was suspect.

Aunt Fern's cell chimed, but being polite, she didn't answer it. "See who it is," I said.

I swear she almost giggled. "Okay." She read the text and grinned. "Dolly just texted that our special guest has agreed to come."

It wasn't long ago that my aunt and Dolly weren't on the best of terms. They were always competing for who ran the most successful restaurant, but they'd since mended that broken fence. I looked over at Jaxson to see if he knew anything about a sixth gossip queen, but he subtly shook his head.

"Are you going to share the name of this special guest?" Jaxson asked.

"It's Gertrude Poole."

Okay, I hadn't expected that. Gertrude was the town's psychic. She also had been training Rihanna to follow in her footsteps someday, and I had to say my cousin was an excellent student. Rihanna's ability to read minds was a bit unsettling, but thankfully, she'd been able to control when she listened and when she didn't. "That's awesome. You ladies will have a great time."

"I hope so." Our food arrived. "I'll leave you two to your meal. I'll see you, Glinda, tomorrow. And Jaxson, enjoy your family time."

"Thanks."

I dug into my food. "I am so happy Aunt Fern will be with friends in a bit," I said once I stopped long enough to take a breath.

"I agree, and I'm equally as glad that we will be together as well. I can't wait for you to open the present I got you."

I'd always spent Christmas Eve with my parents, so being with Jaxson would be extra special. I was also glad my parents would have a quiet evening together for a change. "Can you give me a hint what you got me?"

He chuckled. "Not on your life."

"Fine. Be that way." I tried to act offended, but I'm sure the smile on my face showed I wasn't. For the rest of our meal, we talked about our usual issue of how to drum up new clients for our business. Witch's Cove was a small town, and it wasn't as if someone was murdered every day or every week for that matter. "We need to focus on investigating disappearing relatives, cheating spouses, and such," I said.

Jaxson chuckled. "You'd be bored within the year if that is all we did."

He knew me too well. "I know, but unless we move to a city where there is more crime—which I never will do—that might be all we can do." It was probably why we were the only private investigation firm in town, and Witch's Cove couldn't even support us.

"We'll figure something out."

That was what he always said. When we finished, I tried to pay, but my aunt wouldn't hear of it. "Call it an early Christmas present."

I leaned across the counter and hugged her. "Thank you. You are the best. Have fun with the girls, and I'll see you tomorrow."

After I zipped up my jacket, we walked back to the office so I could pick up Iggy. I needed to head home in order to get ready for my hot date.

When we entered, Iggy was on my desk sniffing the mistletoe. "What are you doing?" I asked.

"I was wondering if I sprinkle some catnip on this stuff if it would work between me and Aimee."

Aimee was my aunt's cat who, by a mistake of magic, was given the ability to talk just like Iggy. Being a cat though, one moment she would pay attention to my familiar, and the next Aimee would ignore him. "Mistletoe is mostly for New Year's Eve, but it can be used any time during the holiday season."

"Use it how?" he asked.

I certainly didn't mind a demonstration. Just as I picked it up, Rihanna came out of her room. "I thought I heard voices."

I was sure she heard more than just our voices. She'd probably read my mind and came out to see the fireworks when I bestowed the toe-tingling kiss on Jaxson. Fine, I'd give her something to see.

I lifted the mistletoe over my head and walked over toward Jaxson. "Iggy wants to understand how this mistletoe works. Watch and learn, people."

I pulled Jaxson's head toward mine with my free hand. The second we kissed, my world spun, and then a bright light swirled around me. The intensity made me feel as if I were falling.

Then everything stopped, and the air was sucked out of the room. I opened my eyes to see if maybe I'd fainted, but what I saw totally and completely stunned me.

Mistletoe and the Pink Bow (book 8 of A Witch's Cove Mystery) is available.

Buy on Amazon or read for FREE on Kindle Unlimited

## THE END

**A WITCH'S COVE MYSTERY** (Paranormal Cozy Mystery)
PINK Is The New Black (book 1)
A PINK Potion Gone Wrong (book 2)
The Mystery of the PINK Aura (book 3)
Box Set (books 1-3)
Sleuthing In The PINK (book 4)
Not in The PINK (book 5)
Gone in the PINK of an Eye (book 6)
Box Set (books 4-6)
The Pink Pumpkin Party (book 7)
Mistletoe with a Pink Bow (book 8)

**SILVER LAKE SERIES (3 OF THEM)**
**(1). HIDDEN REALMS OF SILVER LAKE**
(Paranormal Romance)
Awakened By Flames (book 1)
Seduced By Flames (book 2)
Kissed By Flames (book 3)
Destiny In Flames (book 4)
Box Set (books 1-4)
Passionate Flames (book 5)
Ignited By Flames (book 6)
Touched By Flames (book 7)
Box Set (books 5-7)
Bound By Flames (book 8)
Fueled By Flames (book 9)
Scorched By Flames (book 10)

**(2). FOUR SISTERS OF FATE: HIDDEN REALMS OF SILVER LAKE** (Paranormal Romance)
Poppy (book 1)

Primrose (book 2)
Acacia (book 3)
Magnolia (book 4)
Box Set (books 1-4)
Jace (book 5)
Tanner (book 6)

## (3). **WERES AND WITCHES OF SILVER LAKE**
(Paranormal Romance)
A Magical Shift (book 1)
Catching Her Bear (book 2)
Surge of Magic (book 3)
The Bear's Forbidden Wolf (book 4)
Her Reluctant Bear (book 5)
Freeing His Tiger (book 6)
Protecting His Wolf (book 7)
Waking His Bear (book 8)
Melting Her Wolf's Heart (book 9)
Her Wolf's Guarded Heart (book 10)
His Rogue Bear (book 11)
Box Set (books 1-4)
Box Set (books 5-8)
Reawakening Their Bears (book 12)

## **OTHER PARANORMAL SERIES**
**PACK WARS** (Paranormal Romance)
Training Their Mate (book 1)
Claiming Their Mate (book 2)
Rescuing Their Virgin Mate (book 3)
Box Set (books 1-3)
Loving Their Vixen Mate (book 4)

Fighting For Their Mate (book 5)
Enticing Their Mate (book 6)
Box Set (books 1-4)
Complete Box Set (books 1-6)

**HIDDEN HILLS SHIFTERS** (Paranormal Romance)
An Unexpected Diversion (book 1)
Bare Instincts (book 2)
Shifting Destinies (book 3)
Embracing Fate (book 4)
Promises Unbroken (book 5)
Bare 'N Dirty (book 6)
Hidden Hills Shifters Complete Box Set (books 1-6)

**CONTEMPORARY SERIES**
**MONTANA PROMISES**
(Full length contemporary Romance)
Promises of Mercy (book 1)
Foundations For Three (book 2)
Montana Fire (book 3)
Montana Promises Box Set (books 1-3)
Hart To Hart (Book 4)
Burning Seduction (Book 5)
Montana Promises Complete Box Set (books 1-5)

**ROCK HARD, MONTANA** (contemporary romance novellas)
Montana Desire (book 1)
Awakening Passions (book 2)

**PLEDGED TO PROTECT**
(contemporary romantic suspense)
From Panic To Passion (book 1)
From Danger To Desire (book 2)
From Terror To Temptation (book 3)
Pledged To Protect Box Set (books 1-3)

**BURIED SERIES** (contemporary romantic suspense)
Buried Alive (book 1)
Buried Secrets (book 2)
Buried Deep (book 3)
The Buried Series Complete Box Set (books 1-3)

**A NASH MYSTERY** (Contemporary Romance)
Sidearms and Silk(book 1)
Black Ops and Lingerie(book 2)
A Nash Mystery Box Set (books 1-2)

**STARTER SETS (Romance)**
Contemporary
Paranormal

# Author Bio

Love it HOT and STEAMY? Sign up for my newsletter and receive MONTANA DESIRE for FREE. smarturl.it/o4cz93?IQid=MLite

OR Are you a fan of quirky PARANORMAL COZY MYSTERIES? Sign up for this newsletter. smarturl.it/CozyNL

Not only do I love to read, write, and dream, I'm an extrovert. I enjoy being around people and am always trying to understand what makes them tick. Not only must my romance books have a happily ever after, I need characters I can relate to. My men are wonderful, dynamic, smart, strong, and the best lovers in the world (of course).

My Paranormal Cozy Mysteries are where I let my imagination run wild with witches and a talking pink iguana who believes he's a real sleuth.

I believe I am the luckiest woman. I do what I love and I have a wonderful, supportive husband, who happens to be hot!

# Fun facts about me

(1) I'm a math nerd who loves spreadsheets. Give me numbers and I'll find a pattern.
(2) I live on a Costa Rica beach!
(3) I also like to exercise. Yes, I know I'm odd.

I love hearing from readers either on FB or via email (hint, hint).

## Social Media Sites

**Website:**
www.velladay.com

**FB:**
facebook.com/vella.day.90

**Twitter:**
@velladay4

**Gmail:**
velladayauthor@gmail.com

Printed in Great Britain
by Amazon